THE CAMERA KILLER

THE
CAMERA
KILLER

Thomas
Glavinic

Translated by
John Brownjohn

amazoncrossing 🌐

The Camera Killer was first published in 2003 by 2003 Deutscher Taschenbuch Verlag GmbH & Co. KG, München as *Der Kameramörder*. Translated from German by John Brownjohn. First published in English by AmazonCrossing in 2012.

Published by AmazonCrossing
P.O. Box 400818
Las Vegas, NV 89140

ISBN-13: 9781612183237
ISBN-10: 1612183239
Library of Congress Control Number: 2012938784

THE CAMERA KILLER

I HAVE BEEN REQUESTED to commit everything to paper.

My lady friend, Sonja Wagner, and I took advantage of the Easter holiday to make a trip to West Styria. We live near Linz in the north of Austria. Because my partner comes from the Graz area, we have some acquaintances in Styria. We left home by car on Holy Thursday, having arranged to meet up with various friends at an inn near Graz that afternoon.

In the course of that get-together, my partner consumed an excessive and injurious amount of alcohol (a liter of white wine, six one-ounce shots of tequila, and a questionable amount of beer). Early the next morning, around 5:00 a.m., I had to take a room at the inn and put her to bed.

It was 2:00 p.m. on Good Friday when my partner emerged from her alcoholic stupor. We drove the relatively short distance to our friends, Heinrich and Eva Stubenrauch, who reside at No. 6 Kaibing, 8537 Kaibing. We got there around 3:00 p.m. and received a warm welcome. A snack was prepared for us and, because of the fine weather prevailing, served on a big wooden table outside.

We expressed surprise at the fact that the yard was teeming with cats, twenty-five or thirty of them. Heinrich informed us that the animals were the unwanted property of their landlord, a farmer whose house was only some twenty yards away.

My partner declared that the air and the scenery were glorious and that the snack was doing her sore head good. I had to shoo eight wasps away from my lemonade.

After the snack, it was around 4:00 p.m. and almost as hot as in summer. My partner expressed a wish to go for a walk because it might improve her condition. There were no good walks in the immediate vicinity of Heinrich and Eva's house, so they drove us to a pull-off beside the main road approximately three miles away. Beyond it lay some extensive fields of wheat and corn. Heinrich jokingly remarked that this was the biggest stretch of terrain in the locality uninterrupted by hills. We walked along the farm tracks between the fields, conversing about commonplace topics (our health, the news, and suchlike).

Insects were whirring through the air, crickets chirping. The sun was blazing down with such intensity that I had to don a pink baseball cap inscribed "Chicago" for fear of getting sunburn or even sunstroke. Discounting the sound of insects, absolute silence reigned.

We left the agricultural land behind us and made our way through some tall grass. There was nothing much to be seen, just a lone tree, a few bushes, and something that resembled a building. On approaching, we saw that it was a small, dilapidated house. Heinrich, who had visited this spot once before, knew all about it. Apparently, it was the remains of a farmhouse that had burned down two decades earlier. Rumor had it that arson was involved. The farmer and his wife had perished in the flames.

Superstitious inhabitants of the neighboring village swore that the ruin was haunted and gave it a wide berth. My partner urged us to leave there at once.

Heinrich chaffed her. Did she believe in ghosts? he asked.

She said she'd had an awful feeling even before we reached the spot. Although her thick head might be to blame, she said, the place had a sinister aura. She couldn't account for it, but she felt frightened.

Heinrich cracked a joke. At that, my partner started to tremble all over and ran off. We had no choice but to follow her. Nobody said anything, and we drove back to the Stubenrauchs.

That evening the women made spaghetti Bolognese. While they were busy in the kitchen, Heinrich talked to me about fishing. Now and then, a cat would get into the house, causing him to jump up and chase the animal outside. He told me that the creatures were regular pests and could not be allowed indoors because they made everything dirty and unhygienic.

After supper, we played rummy. During an intermission occasioned by Eva Stubenrauch's need to obey a call of nature, my partner fetched two packets of Kelly's chips from the kitchen.

Heinrich turned on the television and switched to the news channel. The first news item concerned a state visit abroad. The second reported that two children had been murdered in West Styria—an appalling crime, it seemed.

"Large-scale manhunt in progress. The police are seeking a man of medium height, age thirty or thereabouts, who compelled two children of seven and eight to kill themselves by jumping from tall trees and filmed those crimes with a video camera. A third boy, the deceased children's nine-year-old brother, managed to escape. Urgent inquiries are in progress."

Heinrich encouraged the womenfolk, who had now returned, to watch the news. Eva put her hands over her face. My partner said she had never heard of anything so terrible. Heinrich drew our attention to the fact that the town mentioned in the report was located quite close at hand. He claimed to have heard of the family concerned, whose senior member was the local fire chief, and thought he might have seen the father's picture in a regional newspaper. We all expressed surprise that anybody could compel someone else to commit suicide and wondered how such a thing could happen.

It was, therefore, a while before we could re-devote ourselves to our game of cards.

I won a little money, my partner lost some, Eva won a lot, and Heinrich lost heavily. We ate chips and drank red wine, which Heinrich fetched from the cellar at intervals. Since the cellar was accessible only from outside the house and it had started to rain hard that night, he came back wet every time. This gave rise to general amusement. At around 1:30 a.m., when we had been playing for several hours, Eva replaced the cards in their packet. Before we all took our turn in the bathroom to brush our teeth and wash our faces, Heinrich looked at the news channel again to see if there was anything further about the murdered children. There was nothing new, however. I followed my partner upstairs to the second floor where the bedrooms were situated, taking care to step on the wooden treads with a different foot from her.

The next morning, the sun was shining again. We breakfasted outside at the wooden table. The Stubenrauchs had fixed us a lavish breakfast, including salami, several kinds of cheese, eggs, toast, butter, marmalade, crackers, and fruit juice. We voiced our appreciation by praising its quality and expressing our thanks.

The farmer from next door, who was ambling around in grimy blue overalls and a hat too small for him, came over to us from time to time and spoke about the murders committed within such a short distance of us. He said he knew the children's parents, and anyone who did such a thing should be done away with himself. He mimed a hanging as he said this. He spoke in an excessively loud voice, as if he himself or one of those present were deaf.

The farmer's wife, too, came over to us. Seating herself on the bench beside Heinrich, she put her hands on her lap, which was covered with a stained apron, and shook her head and grimaced to convey how shocked she was. My partner, who had finished her breakfast before me, was standing some six feet from the table at this stage, staring silently into space. Eva nodded at the farmer's wife to convey that she shared her opinion.

Everyone sighed. Heinrich, rolling an apple across the bare tabletop, asked if anything more was known about the perpetrator. My partner said she felt thoroughly unwell and couldn't bear to hear this news talked about. Heinrich advised her to put her fingers in her ears. She was being silly, he said, and she ought to be glad it was such a fine day.

The farmer's wife asked Eva if she wanted to accompany her to the Easter food consecration service later on. Eva replied that she couldn't yet say when she would go and told the farmer's wife not to wait for her.

After breakfast, Eva and my partner took it into their heads to play badminton. Heinrich and I were agreeable to this idea but didn't know where to put up the net, which Eva had gotten out, because the twenty-five or thirty stray cats would very probably spoil our game by jumping up, chasing after the shuttlecock, and engaging in other such activities. What was more, we couldn't find any expanse of ground within a suitable radius because a court of adequate size was precluded by encroaching trees and bushes. Heinrich suggested returning to the spot we had visited on our walk the previous day. My partner flatly refused to go there, citing the sinister atmosphere of the place.

Heinrich and Eva hadn't lived in the district long enough to have a detailed knowledge of the area, which confronted us with a problem. Eva hit on the idea of asking the farmer. He directed us to a spot beyond a nearby hill, saying that it would meet our requirements admirably. We made our way there after we had changed into suitable clothes and footwear and Eva had prepared a picnic and packed it in a wicker basket. The latter receptacle also contained a folded blanket. This was because we might want to play singles, so the other two would have the means to relax in comfort.

Heinrich and I erected the net. We warmed up by playing a game without scoring. Then we played a doubles match, changing partners after every game so that everyone played against everyone else. After three and a half hours or so, two of the players—Eva and I—fell prey to exhaustion.

We made our way home, deep in conversation about the most suitable footwear for playing games in. We continued this discussion even after entering the house. I maintained that sneakers were indispensable. Eva kept contradicting me. The healthiest way to play games, she said, was barefoot. She added that the heat had worn her out and she badly needed a shower. Because she had spoken so casually, I failed to grasp that she meant to freshen up on the spot.

To my utter surprise, she stripped off her flimsy red summer dress, and even her bra and panties, in front of me, then stepped into the bathroom shower stall. My response to these activities was to turn away, but I didn't stop talking about our topic of discussion. Given that I was afforded a momentary glimpse of her dark, bikini-waxed pubic hair, this was more easily said than done. I heard the water being turned on. Commenting on the fact that I had averted my gaze, Eva gave it as her opinion that I was being needlessly prudish. When I didn't reply, she quickly raised the subject of the prevailing heat, which was quite incredible. Even insects had already died of heatstroke, she said jokingly.

Having showered, she asked me to hand her a towel. I complied. Our conversation about the sneaker problem seemed to have lapsed, so I left the bathroom whistling the first few bars of the "Radetzky March."

Outside the house, I sat down on a hammock suspended between an apple tree and a cherry tree and waited for my partner and Heinrich to return, which they did after another hour or so. Eva had just completed her preparations for our Easter lunch and brought out plates and cutlery. She served up smoked pork, dyed eggs, bread, and horseradish so strong that everyone at the table shed tears throughout the meal.

Eva drew our attention to a smell of smoke in the air. The first Easter bonfires were being lit. All the farmers in the vicinity were heathens, Heinrich declared. They misused this sacred occasion by seizing the chance to burn their spring prunings, which was legally prohibited on any other day of the year. At least they had burned witches in the old days, said Heinrich, whereas now everything was just an agricultural measure.

After we had chatted for a while (about the temperature, the lack of wind, the unwonted silence—which was only occasionally broken by the meowing of cats and described by my partner, whom Heinrich accused of undue sensitivity, as sinister—and the prospect of more rain that night), Heinrich was reminded of the murders. He wiped his mouth on a floral napkin and went into the house to see the news. Soon after going inside, he opened a window. (Why this wasn't already open was inexplicable—it would have been desirable in view of the heat.) Heinrich called to us that the ticker headline read, "Video camera found—boy makes statement."

Excitedly, he repeated that the police had found the video camera the murderer had used to film his crimes in an autobahn service area. Would these videos be made accessible to the public? he wondered aloud. He thought they would.

My partner disputed this view, arguing that such scenes would not be broadcast on ethical grounds.

Amid laughter, Heinrich thereupon expressed his belief that my partner did not appear to have a full grasp of the realities of the business world, in general, and the ratings war, in particular.

He was right, as usual, my partner replied.

Heinrich withdrew from the window, but he was soon leaning on the sill again. There was some news. The police had reconstructed the almost inconceivable sequence of events with the aid of statements made by the third child, who had escaped.

On Good Friday morning, the man previously described had accosted the three brothers in a clearing in the forest about a mile from their parents' home. In a matter-of-fact and not-unfriendly tone of voice, the stranger informed them that their parents were in his power. It was up to them whether their parents escaped with their lives or whether the boys' behavior would compel him to kill them in a violent and extremely painful manner. The kidnapped boys must do everything he demanded of them, he said.

Just in case they took it into their heads to run away, he would tie one of them—the nine-year-old who later escaped—to himself and, if the other two ran away, put him to death. He expressly mentioned that the cord with which he secured the boy to his belt was two and a half feet in length and ordinarily used for hog-tying.

This done, the man proceeded to film the children and question them. What were their names? How old were they? Which school did they attend, what did their parents do for a living, etc.? The fiend had spent several hours roaming the woods and fields with his weeping victims, questioning and filming them.

He eventually ordered the seven-year-old to climb the tallest tree in the area and got the eight-year-old, who was more agile, to help him. With his older brother's assistance, the little boy managed to attain a height of thirty-five or forty feet. The older boy then had to climb down again. Still with the camera to his eye, the man ordered the little boy to jump.

This is unbelievable, my partner exclaimed.

Heinrich replied that it was true—he had seen on the Internet a detailed eight-page account of it. My partner told him to go on. Heinrich reported that the man had threatened to exterminate the boy's entire family if he didn't jump, beginning with his two brothers. When he continued to hesitate, the man stepped up the pressure and assured him that he would come to no harm; he even promised to catch him. So the little boy eventually jumped and died in consequence. That too was filmed.

At this point, my partner interjected that the killer would soon be caught because his voice was bound to have given him away. She now felt convinced that the video would be shown after all, if only to enable viewers to identify the man by his voice.

This wasn't so certain, Heinrich replied, because the killer had thoroughly disguised his voice by speaking in a hoarse falsetto. He added that, thanks to the enormity of the crime, television crews were converging on West Styria from all over the world. According to the news, Frauenkirchen, the victims' hometown, was under siege. "The Crime Goes Global," ran one headline. A horde of journalists was on the spot, the children's mother had been committed to the Am Feldhof psychiatric institute, and the surviving boy was in an artificially induced coma.

A cry rang out from inside the house, and Eva came hurrying out in tears. She wanted to hear no more of this frightful business, she wailed, her voice breaking. Heinrich must give the subject a rest—she couldn't bear it anymore. She was trembling all over, clenching her fists and sobbing. My partner put her arms around her. Heinrich, who continued to stand at the window, chewed the skin around his fingernails and said no more.

It was eight or ten minutes before Eva could re-devote herself to her hostess's duties (washing up, etc.). My partner told Heinrich it really would be better if he exercised a little restraint where details of this terrible affair were concerned. It was getting on her nerves too—more so than anything she had read in the newspaper or seen on television for a long time.

This remark gave rise to a discussion of whether one was more affected by tragedies that occurred in one's immediate or relatively immediate vicinity than by things that happened far away. Heinrich referred to weeping Yugoslavs and compared them to emaciated Ethiopian children. Another example he cited was an earthquake or volcanic eruption (he couldn't exactly recall which) that had cost fifty thousand people their lives (the toll might have been higher or lower, his memory had failed him yet again). That catastrophe, which had occurred in some remote country in Asia or South America, had scarcely made the news with us. He himself had been far less horrified by it than he was now.

True, said my partner; she also tended to dismiss reports of an earthquake with some indifference, whereas the children's murder had touched her deeply, probably because it had occurred so close at hand.

They were children, Sonja, Heinrich put in; that was an additional factor. I reminded the other two that we perceive tears only if we actually see them and that we have to be familiar with faces in order to be able to sense their pain. That fitted in with Heinrich's theory, I said. Yugoslav faces were more familiar to us than those of swarthy desert dwellers. My partner and Heinrich said I was right.

Silence reigned for a while. All present watched the cats promenading across the yard or lying around and periodically scratching themselves.

My partner remarked that Heinrich hadn't finished his account. Ghastly or not, she wanted to know how the other boy had met his death. Speaking in a low voice so as not to upset his wife again, Heinrich recounted what he had seen on the Internet. He did, however, preface this by mentioning that a special television program would be transmitted from the victims' hometown, which was less than six miles away, in about twenty-five minutes' time. He suggested driving over there. In view of Eva's state of mind, we declined. After a moment's reflection, Heinrich conceded that we were right.

Accordingly, he went on with his account. The dead boy was exhaustively filmed and then left lying in situ. The man shepherded the two surviving children through the forest and interviewed them with special reference to their brother's death. At no point was he ever unfriendly. He didn't hit them, just subjected them to psychological pressure until they yielded to his will and did all he demanded of them.

One particular task the cameraman set them was absurd, Heinrich said. When they were passing an isolated, seldom-used barn containing a small quantity of hay, he ordered them to set fire to the timber building. For this purpose, he turned the hog-tied brother loose. In some manner not described in detail, the killer's threats had rendered the children so submissive that, when the barn was on fire, the older boy submitted to the leash once more instead of trying to escape with the other one. Once the man had filmed the blaze and questioned the surviving brothers about their emotions on camera, they withdrew into the depths of the forest once more.

The second murder was not long in coming. The eight-year-old was made to climb a tall tree. This he did only because the killer threatened to cut off the nine-year-old's ears, underlining the words by holding a knife to his head. Then came a repetition of what had happened in the case of the first brother. The boy on the ground was filmed being asked if he was scared on behalf of his brother up the tree. The latter was also questioned about his feelings and reminded that his parents and his brother would die an incredibly painful death unless he jumped within the next ten minutes. He still had ten minutes—how did that strike him?

What a sadist, my partner put in—what an infamous criminal!

Another eight minutes, said Heinrich—or rather, said the cameraman. Another five. Another three... The camera was not turned off. At zero seconds, the boy jumped.

The silence that followed this account was broken by Heinrich's injunction to watch the special broadcast. Eva refused and remained in the kitchen. The rest of us seated ourselves on the sofa and in an armchair in the living room. We propped our legs on the knee-high coffee table. Heinrich rose and went to get some chips, which he emptied into a big white bowl. He had only just sat down when he had to get up again. The sun was so low that the television screen reflected it and obscured the picture. After Heinrich had blacked out the windows with some drapes lying ready for the purpose, the program began.

The presenter gave a brief summary of what had happened, largely repeating what Heinrich had already told us. He added that the crime had evoked an incredible response, as viewers would shortly be able to see for themselves. Then came some live shots of the bereaved family's hometown. A makeshift platform had been erected in Frauenkirchen's main square and was ringed by thousands of spectators. Standing on it were a woman reporter and the weeping mayor. Easter bonfires were burning in the far distance. The television showed pictures of the crowd. Photographers with flashguns and television cameramen jostled and shouted wildly in its midst as they tried to go about their work.

Just look at this, Heinrich exclaimed—it's insane.

The crowd briefly quieted when the reporter started to speak, but uproar broke out after she had said only a few words. People stormed the platform, thrust the reporter aside, and yelled at the camera, swearing to find the perpetrator and kill him. Everyone was shouting at once. We even heard two gunshots. A camera in an elevated position (possibly the window of a private residence rented for the occasion) panned over the mob until it located the gunman just as he loosed off a third round: An elderly man in hunter's costume and a gray hat fired his rifle in the air. The shot did not, however, have a tranquilizing effect. The crowd continued to yell and rampage and shake their fists in the air with undiminished ferocity, not that it was clear whom their gestures were aimed at.

Just look, just look, Heinrich kept saying, and my partner exclaimed that the whole affair defied belief.

Since the woman reporter had now been swallowed up by the crowd, we were returned to the studio. The presenter said it was incredible what people were capable of. Heinrich wondered aloud if he meant the murderer or the mob. A psychologist was questioned about such details of the crime as were already known. The occupants of the living room promptly agreed that his remarks made no sense.

Cut to the seething mob again. The woman reporter had taken refuge in the mayor's office. There she interviewed Frauenkirchen's leading citizen and other persons who were locally prominent or acquainted with the victims' family. The din in the background was clearly audible.

After that, reports of the hunt for the killer were broadcast from the studio. Various forensic sketches were shown and telephone numbers screened. The presenter stated that a full-scale manhunt had been initiated and several leads were being followed up. The Ministry of the Interior had, however, imposed a news blackout twenty minutes earlier. Viewers were referred to the *News in Pictures* program at 7:30 p.m., but if any significant new development occurred in the next few minutes or hours, the channel would go live.

Heinrich pronounced the program frightful when it ended.

My partner merely shook her head.

The phone rang. With a sigh, Heinrich hurried out into the passage and picked up. Hello, Mother, he said. Yes, he'd already heard, he'd just been watching the program. He returned to the living room carrying the phone, which was equipped with an extension cord. Resuming his seat, he deposited the phone on the coffee table.

In a low voice, my partner asked what could possibly be going on in the heads and hearts of the parents; she dreaded to imagine.

Eva came in. Heedless of the fact that Heinrich was on the phone, she complained of the trouble she would have to go to replace the extension cord behind the bookcase. It was time he got out of the habit of phoning in the living room, she said. Heinrich made a dismissive gesture. Still on the phone, he picked up the remote control with his free hand and switched from channel to channel. Six out of twenty-five channels were currently reporting on the crime in West Styria.

We pricked up our ears when a German commercial station broadcast some dramatic news. It had obtained a leaked copy of the films the criminal had made of his victims. After much internal discussion, the editorial board had decided to televise excerpts from them at some still-to-be-determined time, but in the very near future, in order to give the world a graphic illustration of the enormity of the crime in question.

Heinrich uttered a yell. They're going to show the video, they're going to show the video, he shouted into the receiver and told the person on the other end of the line (presumably his mother) the name of the channel.

He started to hang up but was evidently dissuaded by his interlocutor. No, he said, Eva and he were not going to celebrate Easter in a big way, their visitors had come for a holiday, not for a Christian festival, and no, he wanted some peace and quiet; he definitely wasn't going to Mass, so would the person on the line stop bending his ear about it. The Catholic Church, he declared, was a disgusting bunch of power-hungry hypocrites and pedophiles whose crazy German overlord posed as the representative of some nonexistent being. It might even have been one of his minions that had chased the Frauenkirchen children through the forest with his cassock fluttering, panting as he did so.

Heinrich said a curt good-bye and hung up, swearing to himself.

Eva snatched up the phone and replaced it in its cradle. She also participated in the argument over whether we should watch the murder pictures. Leaning against the doorpost and wringing her hands, she begged Heinrich to spare us.

She might be right, said Heinrich, but he couldn't help it, he simply had to watch them. My partner said she felt the same way. I expressed a similar sentiment.

After some ten minutes' argument, Eva said she would have to watch the program herself. Heinrich waxed indignant. Why talk such nonsense? He wouldn't allow her to watch it—she would have nightmares and so on. She retorted that he was to blame, with his stupid news reports and accounts and descriptions. He had dragooned her into it. Now she wanted to watch it. So saying, she left the room. Heinrich jumped up and followed her out. They could be heard arguing in the kitchen for a while.

My partner and I exchanged glances. I was feeling hungry, so I went into the kitchen to get myself a slice of bread. My appearance put an end to the altercation between Eva and Heinrich. Eva cut me a thick slice of bread with a kitchen knife some ten inches long. Would one be enough? she asked. I nodded.

She opened the refrigerator and asked me what I would like on it. She picked up a salami sausage in her left hand and showed it to me. Transferring it to her right hand, she picked up a lump of Swiss cheese in her left and looked at me inquiringly. Then she replaced the salami in the refrigerator and transferred the cheese to her right hand. With her left hand, she removed a fresh packet of butter (organic, the wrapper said so) from the refrigerator. By passing objects from her left hand to her right in this manner and replacing them in the refrigerator, she was offering me a choice of toppings. I opted for cheese spread.

Eva apologized to me for no reason. This horrible business was getting on her nerves, she said. If her indisposition was blighting the atmosphere, she was sorry and would take care not to do so again.

We went back into the living room, where my partner and Heinrich were discussing the fact that the murders had brought, or would bring, reporters to West Styria from all over the world. This might give the tourist industry a boost, said Heinrich. In this connection, he pointed to the cannibalistic crimes committed by a certain Mr. Dahmer, whom he called a monster without equal. To the best of his knowledge, however, the hunt for Mr. Dahmer and his capture had not aroused as much interest in the media.

My partner objected that injuring, robbing, and murdering other people was commonplace in the United States, so those whose actions transgressed the socially accepted bounds of brutality could not expect to attract much attention there. In a civilized Central European country, by contrast, any murder was of importance, and one such as had occurred yesterday in West Styria was correspondingly sensational.

Eva endorsed this view. She also apologized to my partner.

The latter brushed this aside, but she did express the belief that it was essential not to take the world's misfortunes too hard because this was detrimental to one's own well-being.

The Stubenrauchs now asked what we, being their guests, would like to have for supper. My partner reminded them of our Easter lunch. I begged them not to go to any trouble. Eva said she would like to make us something special. Heinrich and my partner persuaded her not to devote too much time and effort to supper. This would give us an opportunity to engage in activities that were more fun for all concerned (playing games, talking, etc.). Once agreement had been reached (spaghetti Bolognese), we devoted ourselves to the news, unchallenged by Eva.

Austrian Broadcasting's news ticker was reporting that a German commercial station was planning to televise extracts from the murder video. Heinrich remarked that this was the first time ORF had advertised on behalf of a commercial channel. The news reported that the archbishop of Vienna had issued a statement. He appealed to the German TV station not to transmit the projected program because it would not only be an affront to the dead children's memory and human dignity but also have unpredictable consequences on various levels.

Addressing himself to the West Styrian demonstrators, whose numbers were reported to be steadily swelling, he urged them to refrain from physical violence and join with him and the whole of Austria—indeed, with the entire world—in praying for the victims and their parents. The pope himself was praying for the victims, he added. "The holy father has personally assured the children's parents of his profound sympathy and included them in his prayers."

That'll please them, sneered Heinrich.

Re: the possibility of beatification under Benedict XVI: "Members of the clergy have urged that the dead children be be-atified, a suggestion opposed by a leading theologian. The victims have not been dead for long enough, he says."

Reactions from the political parties: "The People's Party speaks of a dark day for Austria. The Freedom Party expresses its belief that such disasters are encouraged by a judicial system overly favorable to offenders and proposes a referendum on the reintroduction of the death penalty. The Greens declare that the government parties have now been proved to have failed in re-spect of psychotherapy and the social services."

The chancellor: "Evil exists. The federal chancellor has stated that evil exists and that it is the duty of the state to protect its citizens."

Heinrich: Yeah, yeah, you loser.

Heinrich spent a while switching from channel to channel. The four persons present found it difficult to coordinate their re-sponse to these reports. A German station was showing live shots of demonstrators gathering outside the studio of the commer-cial station that was planning to televise the murder video in an hour's time. Oh-oh, said Heinrich, and he switched to the murder video channel itself. It made no mention of the demonstrators on its doorstep. Heinrich switched back again.

The woman presenter said that hundreds of police were on their way to protect the TV station and its staff. More and more demonstrators were taking up their positions, armed with plac-ards, signs, and banners. It was uncertain whether they would confine themselves to this noisy but nonviolent expression of opinion.

A police spokesman called it an explosive situation. What could be done to prevent the situation from escalating? he was asked. All he could think of, he replied, was that the station should refrain from televising the tape. He was there to protect the studio, but he ventured to point out that he himself was the father of two children and would like to take this opportunity to send his condolences to Austria. He fully understood the demonstrators' emotions. Things like this should not be shown on television—that, at least, was his personal opinion. There were people employed by the Austrian police who worried him. Far be it for him to prejudge his Austrian counterparts, but only a policeman could have leaked the video to the TV station.

The woman interviewer put her hand to her earpiece. She nodded and said, "More news just in." In view of the mass protests, the broadcaster had agreed to transmit the video at an hour when children were in bed.

Or up a tree or under it, the policeman interjected in a strident voice.

The interviewer went on to say that it had been agreed to transmit the program at 11:30 p.m. In spite of the demonstrations, there was no discernible reason why the transmission should be dispensed with altogether. Certain matters escaped human comprehension; they cried out for pictures.

The policeman shrugged his shoulders. He could offer no guarantees, he repeated several times; the crowd was very heated.

Heinrich clapped his hands. Half past eleven, then! he said.

Eva rose and said she would make supper. My partner followed her into the kitchen. Their argument over whether my partner, being a guest, was entitled to help make the sauce—after all, she said, she had helped Eva the day before—was audible in the living room.

Heinrich searched for other television channels reporting on the murders. There was no more news for a while. Then Austrian television announced in a ticker at the foot of the screen that the federal president intended to address the nation during the *News in Pictures* program at 7:30 p.m. Moreover, the evening program had been changed. In view of the occasion, the Easter Vigil service in St. Stephen's Cathedral would be televised at 10:00 p.m.

Heinrich went into the kitchen to inform the two women. My partner came hurrying into the living room and asked if it were true the federal president would be speaking. I confirmed this. Heinrich, who had come in behind my partner, smiled and called it typical of the man. He made some more derogatory remarks about our head of state and was unsparing with his unkind comments on Austrian Broadcasting's programmers, who were obviously dominated by clerics. It was outrageous of them to transmit Catholic religious services; what he'd like best would be to convert to Islam or Buddhism in protest. Remarking that he felt tremendously overwrought, he stretched out on the sofa.

My partner flitted back into the kitchen in her woolen stockings.

Under the ticker headline "Police cordon off wide area," Heinrich found: "A sizable contingent of police and paramilitaries is currently cordoning off the area around the crime scene. From evidence that cannot be made public, it is suspected that, despite his obviously temporary presence in the Kaiserwald autobahn service area, the perpetrator has not quit the district. A suspicious car or suspicious license number has been identified."

Heinrich asked me if I thought this possible. If he were the killer, he said, he wouldn't have hung around. I pointed out that the man might be a local inhabitant. Also in favor of this was the fact that the victims belonged to the family of a locally prominent individual—namely, the fire chief. It might have been an act of revenge, I said. Heinrich said I had a point.

For fun, he concocted a scenario in which a farmer whose house had caught fire, only to be extinguished too late, had avenged himself in this way. I asked if he was thinking of the farmer who had been dead for two decades and whose gutted house we had visited the day before. Heinrich burst out laughing. Then, wiping the smile off his face, he said the affair was really too serious to joke about. I agreed. He turned off the television.

News in Pictures wasn't on for a while yet, he said, so would I care to play a game of table tennis with him? I agreed. Having informed the womenfolk of our decision, we carried our drinks—beer in Heinrich's case, apple juice in mine—up to the table tennis room on the second floor. We had to turn on the light because the windows on the second floor of the Stubenrauchs' house were smaller than those on the first.

As I had the night before, I found while climbing the stairs that the smell of mildew permeating the whole of the Stubenrauchs' home (probably attributable to the building's age and poor insulation) was stronger in the table tennis room than in the bedrooms or downstairs. This did not, however, inhibit us from playing several games. Although variable, their outcome eventually proved beyond doubt that Heinrich's proficiency at table tennis was superior to my own. He beat me 21:12, 23:25, 21:12, 21:13. It was then time to go downstairs again so as not to miss the news.

As we made our way along the passage, my partner called from the kitchen that we were just in time, the meal would be served in a few minutes. Before complying with Eva's request to set the table, Heinrich said he must shut up the house first; he had no wish to be disturbed by an illicit invasion of cats during the broadcast or the meal.

While he was shutting every imaginable form of access, I went into the kitchen and complimented Eva on the favorable culinary aroma pervading the house. Eva replied that she was glad and hoped the meal would taste as good as it smelled.

Having shut the cats out, Heinrich opened a wooden kitchen cabinet some six feet high and three wide containing tableware.

Having taken out four plates, he pulled open a drawer and removed cutlery and napkins. These he conveyed to the living room.

I inquired if there was any possibility of making myself useful. Eva handed me a salad bowl, which I carried into the living room and deposited in the center of the table. The bowl contained corn and chicory salad with sliced radishes, chives, shaved gherkins, and pumpkinseed oil and vinegar. I performed my task promptly.

After that, I received permission to wait in an armchair in the living room for the meal to be served. Heinrich had lit a cigarette. My partner reproved him, saying that there was too little time before supper to smoke a whole cigarette. He replied that he would stub it out as soon as the food was on the table. This occurred soon afterward.

Eva put two casseroles on the table, one containing spaghetti, the other Bolognese sauce. She filled each plate in turn, first with spaghetti, then with sauce. Last of all, she sprinkled them with Parmesan cheese. We wished each other *bon appétit.*

Scarcely had we eaten a few mouthfuls when the *News in Pictures* program began, accompanied by even more dramatic background music than usual. With the exception of the weather and sports, all the headlines and forthcoming reports related to the murders in West Styria. The federal president was shown, captioned: "President." A helicopter shot of the victims' hometown: "Noose around Killer Tightens." Pictures of weeping men and women: "Horror-struck." Then the presenter introduced the program. All the facts were recapitulated.

Heinrich pointed out that if the killer were a local man (which the report did not, at least, exclude), he might well be in the vicinity. We should bear that in mind, he said. My partner shushed him for fear of missing something, but she then said she dreaded to consider such a possibility. Half in jest, she advised Heinrich to make sure the front door was locked. With an inscrutable expression, he said it was. Eva had checked, and it was double locked.

Heinrich turned the sound down. He thought it unlikely that the killer, if he were an outsider, would be in the vicinity. Even if he were, he would hardly come here, not even if he was a local man.

My partner said he seemed to doubt his own words; the look on his face gave him away.

Heinrich admitted to feeling uneasy, but there was no danger. There were four of us, including two men—we would make mincemeat of the fellow. Besides, the farmer next door might be elderly, but he was tough and strong. The murderer was welcome to come, he said. When my partner pointed out that he was presumably a psychopath, and one could never tell what one was up against and what such a person was capable of, Heinrich brushed this aside with a belligerent gesture and said that no amount of insanity would be proof against the sturdy arms of those present.

My partner asked what would happen during the night. What if the killer managed to sneak in unobserved while our sturdy arms were relaxing? Heinrich asked if she was genuinely frightened. Not frightened, exactly, my partner replied, but she didn't feel too good.

Heinrich contrived to cheer her up by jocularly assuring her that he and I would take turns to stand guard. He turned the sound up again.

A report on the demonstrations outside the commercial station was just in progress. The transmission of the video was irrevocably scheduled for 11:30 p.m. The presenter mentioned that German politicians had appealed for calm and asked the station to practice restraint. This had failed to have the desired effect on those in charge. Someone—Heinrich coughed just as his name was mentioned, so I missed it—had called for a ban on the transmission, but this too had come to nothing for various reasons.

A spokesman for the TV channel had stated that, although they had the deepest respect for the victims' family and the dead children themselves, the transmission was essential in order to acquaint the public with the full extent of the tragedy. It would be wrong to allow a potential ban to sweep the details under the carpet. The broadcasters refused to be intimidated by threats.

They're talking bullshit, Heinrich exclaimed.

The *News in Pictures* presenter stated that Austrian Broadcasting dissociated itself from such methods and would confine itself to showing a photograph of the victims. The children appeared for the first time. They had a black bar over their eyes, and the photograph was grainy and out of focus. The caption at the foot read, "Franz (seven)" and "Josef (eight)."

This is terrible, Heinrich exclaimed, quite terrible. My partner indignantly agreed. Eva, with her eyes fixed on her plate and a last forkful of spaghetti in her hand, said she meant what she'd said: If this video were televised, all hell would break loose.

What did she mean? inquired my partner.

Heinrich called for silence; the president was coming. Sure enough, the federal president was shown delivering a brief address. The occupants of the living room accompanied it with tokens of disapproval and offensive remarks about the head of state. While a majority of those present were still accusing him of being a disagreeable individual, the studio called its correspondent in West Styria.

The nature of the situation there hadn't changed. The local correspondent, looking down on the crowded main square, commented on this as follows: "Public sentiment is at boiling point." She reported that the bishop of the Graz-Seckau diocese had gone to see the bereaved family an hour earlier. Scheduled for 11:30, doubtless as a mark of disapproval aimed at the abhorrent video transmission, was a memorial service that senior ecclesiastical dignitaries and members of the government were expected to attend.

Meantime, some eight thousand to ten thousand people had converged on a town whose population normally numbered only eight hundred. There was a never-ending stream of cars and buses, camera crews, journalists, and garden-variety rubbernecks. The parish priest, who spoke last, said that God had shut his eyes to them.

Back in the studio, the woman presenter announced some program changes occasioned by current events. At 8:15, there would be a live report from the hard-hit West Styrian town. Thereafter, at around 9:00 p.m., a program on the psyche of murderers first transmitted nine months earlier, and at 10:00 p.m., the Easter Vigil service from St. Stephen's Cathedral in Vienna.

Finally, the commentary turned to the killer. He was around six feet and had dark hair and dark eyes. You bet some viewers will now be shouting that he's a foreigner, said Heinrich.

The presenter: According to the testimony of the boy who escaped, he was roughly thirty years old. However, she went on, experts considered this information unreliable because children possess only a limited ability to estimate an adult's age. Ergo, the man might equally be twenty or forty-five. Two different forensic sketches were shown again. One had been based on the testimony of the surviving child, the other on that of a farmhand who claimed to have spotted a man near the murder scene.

Heinrich said they were as alike as Michael Jackson and Oliver Hardy.

The presenter: The trail wasn't red-hot, but there were some promising leads; that was all that had filtered through the Ministry of the Interior's news blackout.

A new picture appeared beside her. It showed a cordoned-off clearing in the forest, together with some policemen in uniform or scene-of-crime vests. A timetable was inserted. The presenter reported that, on the morning of the day of the murders, an unknown man had captured three children in a forest near the small West Styrian town of Frauenkirchen. In the course of several hours, during which he interviewed them in front of a video camera, two terrible crimes occurred, in addition to the torching of a hay barn. By means of threats and appalling psychological intimidation, the man had induced two of the three boys to throw themselves off tall trees, as a result of which both had died. The third had managed to escape in an unusual manner.

Having questioned him long and exhaustively about his emotional response to the death of his brothers, the killer had offered him a choice. He himself would shut his eyes and count up to a hundred. The boy was at liberty to run away during that time. If he decided to escape, the man would pursue him and, if he caught him, kill him in an extremely brutal fashion, ripping out his nails and flaying him alive, etc. If he failed to catch him, he would turn up on a certain day in the fall and exterminate the boy's entire family, him included. If the boy decided to stay, on the other hand, the man promised him a quick and painless death and his parents' lives would be spared.

The man closed his eyes and began to count slowly. The boy ran off.

A motorist, who spotted the utterly frantic victim several miles from his parental home, picked him up and took him to the police.

Eva kneaded her brow and said she might have to be sick. Heinrich too detected a certain pallor on the faces of all present. He turned off the television. Nobody spoke for five minutes or so.

My partner went over to some shelves on the wall. After a while, she removed a CD and inserted it in the stereo system. Music was a good idea, said Heinrich. He suggested playing a game of cards. Eva said she was far from in the mood for cards, but in view of the circumstances, and because simply doing nothing would probably prevent her from shaking off her horrific thoughts, she was prepared to play. My partner and I did not decline to join in either.

Heinrich fetched the deck of cards from an old wooden sideboard and put it on the table. When he went to get some red wine from the cellar, he discovered how hard it had started to rain again and swore repeatedly. On returning from the cellar with the wine, he remarked that the rain would probably have dispersed the crowd in the victims' hometown. The storm was growing steadily worse, he said.

Eva asked him to drop the subject for a while.

As he was uncorking the wine, my partner opened a drawer in the table and took out some paper and writing utensils. Eva proceeded to shuffle the cards. We played rummy, as we had the previous night. There was no great change in our respective fortunes either, except in the case of Heinrich and myself. I won even more this time, and he lost more heavily than before.

Once again, there were one or two breaks in play. Heinrich, who refused to comply with our suggestion that he bring up more than one bottle at a time (going down there kept him sober, he claimed), had to pay several visits to the cellar. We expressed our belief that he would be bound to catch a cold, even though he put on a blue terry cloth bathrobe after every sortie and changed back into outdoor clothes only when going to the cellar. Eva, who suffers from a weak bladder, had to make frequent visits to the bathroom.

My partner fetched some nibbles and cookies. On one occasion, she went to get a cardigan because the downpour and the open window had made it unpleasantly chilly. During one of these intermissions, when Eva was in the bathroom, Heinrich asked if we believed that the video would really be shown. Neither of us doubted it. He said he insisted on watching the program. We said the same. Eva, who had rejoined us, put her fingers in her ears. Heinrich laughed and said, OK, OK.

There was a knock at the door. My partner gave a violent start. Heinrich rose and we followed him. Standing outside were the farmer from next door and his wife, who was carrying an umbrella. She asked if we were coming with them to Mass at Kaibing Church.

Heinrich was about to reply but was dissuaded by a warning glance and a surreptitious nudge from Eva. No, he said, we weren't going to church but would watch the Easter Vigil Mass on television instead. He felt sure his neighbors were aware that the pope's *Urbi et Orbi* benediction extended to viewers seated in front of their television sets. This was now valid for Easter Vigil services as well. That being so, we would stay home and be blessed by the cardinal on the screen.

Oh, said the farmer's wife, so that's how it was these days. Everything had been different in the old days, and she adhered to the churchgoing tradition. The neighbors took their leave and we returned to the living room.

That passed off all right for once, said Eva, but only just.

Heinrich fulminated about rural traditions and the prevailing compulsion to defer to the Church. Eva said he should drop the subject.

Heinrich went and fetched another bottle of wine. He had to slip into the bathrobe again on his return.

My partner remarked that the rain was getting heavier and heavier. We confirmed this. The rain was thundering down on the old house so loudly that my partner shivered, drew the cardigan around her more tightly, and leaned against me as if in search of protection. Heinrich asked if she was scared of thunderstorms. No, she replied, but the combination of a heavy downpour and a psychopathic murderer roaming around on the loose created an atmosphere that transcended the bounds of normalcy. If there were another knock, Heinrich shouldn't open the door so unthinkingly; she hoped he hadn't forgotten to lock it after his last trip to the cellar. She was assured that it was securely locked.

Eva urged us to go on with our game and, above all, not to widen the discussion. At around 10:15, I went to the bathroom. When I returned to the living room, my partner and Eva were standing, talking beside the kitchen dresser. They were clearly visible to me because the passage connecting the living room and kitchen was short and straight. Heinrich was seated in front of the television, looking at the news. I perched on the arm of my chair.

Heinrich said public holidays were a mystery to him; he'd thought there weren't any newspapers on Easter Sunday. I told him I shared that view, but Heinrich said the *Kronen Zeitung* was bringing out an edition containing an illustrated sixteen-page report on the murders; it had just been advertised. Perhaps it was just a one-time edition, I said. Heinrich promised to go and get a copy by car early tomorrow morning. Unfortunately, the nearest newsstand was situated several miles away. That was one of the disadvantages of living in such a remote spot.

He called to the women in the kitchen, asking where they'd gotten to. We could go on with our game, he said. When there was no response, he went to persuade them to return. I followed him out, so I witnessed Eva reproaching Heinrich for giving the murder story no rest. She didn't feel like going on with the game as long as the remote control was within his reach.

Laughing, Heinrich promised not to turn it on again until 11:30, even though we would, with such tragic finality, have missed the wonderful televised Mass. We were heretics, he said; we hadn't even had our food consecrated.

Eva was about to reply when we heard a crash upstairs. We all stared at each other.

What was that? my partner exclaimed.

Heinrich shrugged his shoulders.

There's someone up there, my partner cried loudly.

Before we could respond in any way, she reiterated her cry of alarm and dashed to the front door. She turned the key twice and wrenched it open, evidently intending to leave the house just as she was, dressed only in a cardigan, T-shirt, and jeans with panties underneath, and wearing no shoes on her stocking feet.

Heinrich restrained her. She mustn't go imagining things, he said; there was no one upstairs, but if it would reassure her, he'd go and look. My partner did, in fact, come to a halt. She even locked the door again, but she refused to leave the spot.

Heinrich went to a medium-sized chest in the passage and took out a flashlight because he might have to go up into the loft, which had no electric light installed. Did he mean to go up there by himself? my partner demanded. Was he crazy?

Heinrich answered the first question in the affirmative, the second in the negative.

I offered to accompany him. My partner said she wouldn't let me; it might be better to call the police and enlist their help. Heinrich told her not to be ridiculous. The police quickly became overburdened with such calls and unable to perform their proper duties in a regulation manner.

To simplify the situation, I suggested that all four of us go; that way, no one need be worried about anyone else.

What gives you that idea? my partner demanded; she would be all the more worried about herself and everyone else. No one and nothing would induce her to go up there. She would sooner summon help from the authorities. Even if this step might seem ridiculous in normal times, the guardians of the law would surely sympathize with such fears on a day like this and might even be grateful for information that could lead to the killer's capture.

Heinrich vigorously contested this. He had no intention of making himself look a fool in front of the police. He was going to have to live here for a long time. Did he want to be known at the police station as the idiot who'd called the police because of a creaking beam? No, he certainly wasn't going to run that risk. So saying, he made for the stairs leading to the second floor.

However, my partner prevented him from carrying out his intention of investigating the mysterious crash on his own. Stirring from the spot for the first time since her abortive attempt to escape, she caught hold of the belt around his bathrobe. He wasn't going up there on his own, she said; she wouldn't allow it.

Heinrich came to a standstill, although his physical superiority would undoubtedly have enabled him to shake off the restraint. He burst out laughing.

She didn't find it funny, Eva said indignantly. Something had to be done. That noise just now really did defy rational explanation. Perhaps they ought to enlist the help of the farmer and his wife.

That was all he needed, Heinrich exclaimed. What was this—blind panic coupled with stupidity? Besides, he doubted their neighbors were back from church yet. The two women should compel themselves to view the situation in a levelheaded manner.

For a while, we all remained where we were in the passage, my partner still clinging to Heinrich's belt. We strained our ears and thought it over.

Eva wanted to discuss the matter as unemotionally as possible, she said. Heinrich would probably not encounter anything dangerous up there, but a certain risk remained. What did he propose to do if, contrary to expectation and mathematical probability, he suddenly found himself confronted by the camera killer in a second-floor room? He possessed immense physical strength, it was true, but the murderer would certainly take advantage of the surprise element. He might be lurking behind a door and attack him unexpectedly. Heinrich should at least be armed. She was thinking of a kitchen knife.

Heinrich retorted that he was not adept at knifeplay and that resorting to such a dubious weapon could very quickly rebound on an unskilled defender. Eva sternly enjoined him to take the matter more seriously.

After reflecting for a moment, Heinrich sighed and agreed to take an ax with him for purposes of self-defense. Eva applauded that decision. My partner, on the other hand, looked worried and would not be weaned from her proposal that we call the police for assistance. Heinrich rejected this, tapping his forehead.

When my partner learned that fetching the ax would first entail another visit to the cellar, she wouldn't hear of it. She made a lightning dash for the telephone, and Heinrich had some difficulty in wresting the receiver from her grasp and hauling her away from the handset. She loudly pointed out the dangers of a trip to the cellar: how easy it would be for the murderer, if he were outside, to capture him and, possibly, start filming.

To resolve the situation, I expressed my full approval of Heinrich's suggestion. Partly ignoring my partner's resistance and partly neutralizing it by exerting physical strength, I opened the door for Heinrich and locked it behind him.

While waiting, Eva and I spoke soothingly to my partner. She abandoned the idea of phoning the police after Eva had argued that such a call might shed an adverse light on her mental state.

There was a knock, and I opened the door without hesitation. Attired in his bathrobe, which was sodden with rain, Heinrich entered, ax in hand. He wasted no time in going upstairs. I followed him. The women plucked up their courage and climbed the stairs too.

Once on the second floor, we turned on the lights in one room after another but found nothing suspicious or out of the ordinary. That left the loft. My partner said she wasn't going up there and made a final attempt to dissuade us from searching it.

If he heard the word *police* one more time, cried Heinrich, he would forget himself and fetch his video camera or do some other nasty things.

Having already climbed the narrow ladder ahead of me, he opened the hatch with his free hand and reached behind him. I passed him the flashlight. Before he plunged his head into the darkness of the loft, he uttered several thunderous challenges. Anyone there? he called. No answer.

The pattering of the rain could be heard at considerably greater volume, and we were enveloped in a cold draft. Eva and my partner remained standing at the foot of the ladder. Heinrich played his flashlight over the loft. It took us a while to solve the mystery: Via some secret route, two cats had succeeded in sheltering there from the storm. Once in the loft, they had evidently romped around. In the course of their cavorting, an open bookcase containing all manner of jumble had fallen over. This was what had caused the crash. When we transmitted this news to the women on the ladder below, it was greeted with hilarity.

Meantime, I briefly devoted my attention to the unusual appearance of one of the cats, which was endeavoring to hide from the beam of the flashlight: It was dressed up. I pointed this out to Heinrich, who laughed. During a family visit a few days ago, he told me, Eva's nephews had asked her grandmother for some clothes for the cats. The old woman in question had given them a few crocheted garments, and the animal in front of us had drawn the short straw.

Let's go back downstairs, he said.

Although the situation had resolved itself satisfactorily, there was something sinister about a pitch-dark loft with the beam of a flashlight playing over it, especially at this juncture.

Heinrich took the flashlight from me and shone it on his wrist. His watch said 11:20. Setting foot on the ladder, he communicated that fact to the women below and urged them to get a move on.

With considerable vehemence, Eva gave vent to her mixed feelings about our forthcoming viewing of the murder video and voiced the hope that the relevant TV station had since been shut down by the police or stormed by demonstrators. Even though the latter procedure violated the principles of constitutional government and represented a criminal offense, she would nonetheless sympathize with the raiders and fully approve of their action.

Heinrich told her to stop bleating.

It fell to me, being the last one down, to shut the hatch to the loft and secure it with a metal bolt. This I did without delay.

On reaching the first floor, we dispersed to complete sundry preparations before the program began. Eva paid another visit to the bathroom. Heinrich temporarily stowed the unused ax in the hall closet and exchanged his wet bathrobe for some dry indoor clothes.

In the kitchen, my partner took a tray some three feet long and two wide from a small cupboard. On this, she placed three packets of Soletti pretzels, two packets of chips, a small bowl of peanuts, four far-too-meager portions of vanilla ice cream, four packets of wafer cookies, and a clean ashtray. I watched her meanwhile.

Heinrich called loudly from the living room that it was 11:28. The program had already started, but not the video yet. We hurried into the living room and took our places. Eva's attempt to thank my partner for her efforts with the food was nipped in the bud by a harsh rebuke from Heinrich, who, lolling on the sofa with his legs crossed, urged us to devote our attention to the screen.

A blonde, overweight presenter was currently conversing with a bearded man of about fifty, the latter being described by a subtitle as a psychologist and theologian. The anchorwoman thanked him for his remarks, then turned to face the camera and addressed the viewers. "Ladies and gentlemen," she said, "a terrible thing has happened, and it is still unclear what such a monstrous crime, which holds us all spellbound, may lead to."

Gingerly opening a box lying on the table in front of her, the anchorwoman said that nothing seemed more illustrative of the world's sense of outrage than the contents of that receptacle, which had been sent to the studio with a request to use it either on the murderer or, in the event that he could not be caught and they really intended to screen this frightful video, on those in charge. As she spoke, she removed from the box a rope with a noose whose manifest purpose was to encircle a throat and bring about the death of its owner.

People are beyond belief, said Heinrich.

The theological psychologist seated beside the presenter came into view once more. He was staring at the noose, shaking his head, and expressing his stupefaction by muttering and gesturing helplessly.

Heinrich: That's the theologian; before, it was the psychologist.

My partner: People are thoroughly evil.

There followed a contribution on the finding of the video. The gas station attendant who had discovered the tapes and camera was interviewed in the Kaiserwald autobahn service area. He pointed out the spot with his forefinger. Even we found it difficult to understand what he was saying in his Styrian dialect, and the German station supplied a subtitled translation.

Some character, said Heinrich.

The presenter said the station had drafted a statement about the forthcoming transmission, and she was now going to read it. Heinrich said she could stuff her statement; he wanted to see the video. Reading from a sheet of paper, the presenter said the TV station was fully aware of its responsibilities. This was precisely the reason for its decision to screen the video. The subject would be dealt with sensitively.

It was 11:43 already, Heinrich exclaimed, so what was all this crap?

Reading on, the presenter said it was time to put an end to American conditions in Europe. This case in Austria, Germany's immediate neighbor, was of concern to everyone. A mirror must be held up in front of society, and the station was shouldering this responsibility.

Heinrich said the presenter was talking utter bullshit, and my partner endorsed this. The only one of us not to have eaten his ice cream, Heinrich picked up his bowl.

The video would be screened very soon, said the presenter. First, however, in case anyone felt the need to consult an expert after watching the videos, the telephone numbers of some psychological advice centers would be shown. This service was free, barring a maximum telephone charge of €0.50 per minute. After a short commercial break, the video would begin. The telephone numbers were inserted.

Shortly thereafter, viewers were treated to the sight of a young woman being enjoined by her two little boys to purchase a certain cream-filled candy bar. Heinrich indignantly remarked that the programmers were taking their time with a vengeance. He switched channels.

The next channel was just reporting on the demonstration outside the transmitter of the murder video. Despite the lateness of the hour, hundreds of people were besieging the television studio. Their banners were inscribed with vulgar abuse. One of them expressed the belief that the TV station had commissioned the murders itself and paid for the films in advance. Some bore the words "Snuff Pigs" or "Snuff Killers" and "You Peddle Snuff."

Eva asked what *snuff* meant. Heinrich explained that snuff videos were films that recorded real-life murders and that there was a special market for these. Eva said she'd heard of them. It only went to show how sick the world really is, my partner remarked.

Heinrich disputed this. During the Middle Ages, people had been beheaded in public, and the spectators, who turned out in force, had thoroughly enjoyed the sight. We were no better than the people of those days.

But we used to be better once upon a time, my partner retorted.

Heinrich shrugged his shoulders and switched back to the murder video channel. It was still showing commercials, a fact on which Heinrich commented adversely. It was 11:52, he said; were they going to take all night about it and end by singing the praises of Gigantico's Super-Duper, Lightning-Fast Vacuum Cleaner?

Then he suggested filling in the time with another game of cards. My partner opposed this idea, citing our excessive nervous tension in expectation of the video. Heinrich bet me the video wouldn't be shown before midnight. I accepted the bet and won.

At 11:58 the plump anchorwoman reappeared. She announced that the video would now be screened. Approximately four hours' material was available. The channel had edited it down and would transmit the crucial scenes, or scenes that encapsulated the entire course of events. Any children and adolescents under the age of sixteen now watching the screen should be sent out of the room by those responsible for their upbringing.

Heinrich jokingly ordered his wife out of the room, but Eva didn't consider this funny.

From one moment to the next, the quality of the images on the screen changed. A digital clock was running in the top right corner of the picture. In the first scene, it showed 0:08. This signified that the first seven minutes had been deemed unworthy of transmission. An informative ticker at the foot of the screen read, "Screening this video is not sensationalism. It is a vain attempt to come to terms with an incomprehensible human tragedy."

Incredible, said Heinrich, plunging his hand in the bowl of peanuts. Eva chewed her nails and directed only occasional glances at the screen. My partner said she failed to understand why anyone would do such things, let alone film them, and why any TV station would show them. Heinrich shushed her and pointed at the screen, which was showing a patch of forest.

The camerawork was jerky. The cameraman was moving forward. We saw a clearing in which three children were racing around with sticks in their hands.

Cut. 0:15. A high-pitched, distorted voice—that of the cameraman—informed them that now one of them was his prisoner, he doubted the others would be rash enough to run away. Any such attempt would cost the lives, first of the remaining boy and then, within a few hours at most, of the other two and all the members of their family.

He took them completely by surprise, said Heinrich.

The hog-tied brother came into the shot. He asked the man why he was doing this to them. The camera panned. The boy who was second in age repeated that he wanted to leave and the man should let them all go. Heinrich urged us to look at his expression, which was alternating between an uncertain smile and undisguised fear. He didn't seem to fully grasp the situation or believe in its gravity. Only ten minutes earlier, Heinrich added, they had been romping around unsuspectingly, and even now, they probably thought they'd be playing tag again in another quarter of an hour.

The hoarse voice asked the youngest boy what he would think if he, the cameraman, slit open his hog-tied brother's stomach to see if his innards smoked like the cigarettes the grown-ups smoked at home or steamed like food on the table. The cameraman said this was so, he knew it. It also smoked or steamed when you did a pee outside, if it was cold enough.

What's he on about? Heinrich exclaimed.

The children didn't answer.

The cameraman went on to describe several other ways of torturing someone. This speech, of which the children took note with unmistakable distaste, evoked exclamations of an indignant nature from all present in the living room.

The cameraman never stopped filming the children for an instant. This gave us an opportunity to study their changing expressions. They don't have a clue, Heinrich exclaimed, not a clue.

The boy who was clearly the youngest of the three had already burst into tears some time ago. Whimpering and hopping up and down on the spot in a silly way—and, interestingly enough, clutching his genitals—he requested the cameraman to release him and his brothers from their disagreeable predicament.

After that, the camera panned to the second of the three in age. His hair, which had not been cut for some time, hung down over his eyebrows. The camera voice asked him if it would give him pleasure to see the brains of his brothers or parents. To this, the boy replied in the negative. He also rejected the suggestion that he might like to thrust the whole of his hand into their backs or abdominal cavities.

The cameraman then said that, this being so, the brothers must at all costs comply with every one of his instructions. The least recalcitrance would compel him to take one of them and cut off his nose or a finger and put salt on the wound, thereby doing the boy in question harm.

By now, all three children were in tears. The cameraman's remarks had also caused uproar in the living room. The gap between the seven-year-old's front teeth was clearly visible in close-up. He never stopped crying. This prompted the man behind the camera to warn the boys that they must not interrupt the proceedings by indulging in exaggerated emotional outbursts. In particular, it was imperative that they answer his questions. Their replies must not be impaired by sobbing or vocal distortions occasioned by despair.

A cut ensued. The clock in the top right corner of the screen now showed 0:48.

Eva helped herself to a heaped handful of chips. Some of them escaped from her fingers and cascaded down her white T-shirt, which bore the legend, "Morning Star." Heinrich called her a greedy pig. Eva greeted this jocular rebuke expressionlessly and without looking at anyone.

The cameraman was just instructing the gap-toothed brother to climb a tree.

Oh no, said Eva, here it comes.

The boy jibbed. He complied only when the camera voice explained that having his abdominal cavity slit open and then salted would be an extremely unpleasant experience for his hog-tied brother to undergo and that this would be promptly put into effect in the event of further resistance on his part. Bawling, he climbed the tree with the second brother's assistance. The camera also recorded his ascent.

Once he had reached the top of the tree and the other boy had returned to the ground, the camera voice instructed him to jump when ordered to. The resulting cries of anguish and protest from the treetop were graphically illustrated by a close-up. Then the camera panned to the hog-tied boy. The man asked him how it felt to know that his brother was about to rejoin them in free fall and what his chances of survival would be after a descent from approximately forty-five feet.

The hog-tied boy wept. He referred to the possibility of vengeance on the part of his father, whom he claimed to be extremely tall and strong. The cameraman took note of this with evident interest. He asked exactly what his father would do on receiving news of his brother's death, not forgetting to add that this question possessed only theoretical importance. Why? Because his father would meet an even more terrible fate unless the brothers obeyed every order given them by him, the cameraman, to his complete satisfaction.

He also asked the long-haired boy how it felt to be about to lose a brother.

It felt quite awful, was the reply. Wasn't there any way of preventing this adverse development? There was one, the cameraman responded: The going rate for a brother's life was one eye. The long-haired boy must poke out his hog-tied brother's eye with a stick—not with a single thrust, but by drilling it out good and proper. The boy thus addressed replied that he didn't want to do this and made a renewed plea to be released from captivity, together with his brothers. This request was rejected.

The cameraman then asked the gap-toothed brother how he proposed to jump. Would he push off vigorously with his legs or simply fall? One should always opt for the elegant as opposed to the ungraceful, he said. Whimpers were the sole response.

The cameraman inquired about (a) the view from the tree and (b) the prospect of leaping to one's death. For the umpteenth time, the boy up the tree screamed that he was feeling ill and would rather not jump. The man commanded him to do so and instructed him to perform a telemark, like a ski jumper.

Eva rose, saying she couldn't watch this. Her statement was registered in silence by the rest of those present. She set off in the direction of the kitchen. A moment later, we heard the sound of running water.

Weeping, the gap-toothed brother shook his head. This the cameraman took as an occasion to mention the knife in his hand (it was not visible), compel the hog-tied brother to bare his stomach, and call to the boy in the tree that the unpleasant operation was imminent and the salt ready and that today would demand exceptional efforts on the cameraman's part because, if the gap-toothed boy persisted in his refusal, he would have to operate on his mother's stomach and spine as well.

After the order to jump had been repeated several times, a scream was heard from one of the children on the ground. The camera voice croaked that the operation would commence in ten seconds, so he must jump. Nothing would happen to him. If he didn't, he would render everything still worse and more painful.

Five, four, three, two, one, counted the man.

Then we saw a shiny red sports car. After a moment's surprise, we realized we were being treated to a commercial break.

I don't believe this, Heinrich muttered.

My partner sighed and reached for the Soletti without a word.

We stared, unspeaking, at the screen for a good ten minutes. Eva came in and asked if it was over. On being told that the program would resume after the commercial break, she returned to the kitchen.

At last, we were back in the clearing. The man was counting: Five, four, three, two, one… On zero, the gap-toothed boy jumped, accompanied by the camera and his brothers' cries of horror.

Suddenly, the screen went black. A dull thud was heard.

Some of those present in the living room groaned when the picture reappeared. The camera approached the gap-toothed boy, who was lying motionless on the ground. Before it went into close-up, there was another fade-out.

In the next scene, the clock in the corner of the screen said 1:31. The channel once more informed us by ticker that screening this video was not sensationalism, but a vain attempt to come to terms with an incomprehensible human tragedy.

The surviving boys were interviewed about their thoughts and feelings in respect of their brother's demise. They did, however, display total passive resistance. This prompted Heinrich to remark that they might have been prepared to speak but were too traumatized to do so. My partner endorsed this view by slowly inclining her head.

We witnessed the long-haired brother vomiting.

My partner rose, saying she'd had quite enough of what we had seen so far and would sooner keep Eva company in the kitchen. She was feeling sick, she declared, and incapable of continuing to watch what was happening on the screen.

After she had left the room, Heinrich hurried over to some wooden shelves whose highest point was a half inch short of the ceiling and took out a videocassette. This he inserted in the appropriate video recorder, which was beneath the television set. He said he thought it fitting to respect the women's sensitivity. Interested though he was in the subsequent course of events, he couldn't disregard their desire for de-escalation. He would therefore record the rest of the program and we would watch it at a later stage, possibly with Eva and my partner, should they have recovered their mental equilibrium by then. I concurred with his assessment of the situation and expressed my approval of his course of action.

Once Heinrich had set the requisite controls, he turned the video machine on (the long-haired brother was still being sick) and the television off. I followed him into the kitchen. There he put his arms around Eva, who was crying. I took a green-and-red apple from the dresser and cut it in two. One half I sank my teeth in, the other I handed to my partner, who took my offering without a word. She directed some consoling remarks at Eva, then silence fell.

Heinrich broke it by suggesting a doubles at table tennis in order to steer our thoughts into different channels. Eva objected that she wasn't currently capable of amusing herself in such a fashion. This prompted Heinrich to demand, in a peremptory tone of voice, that she cease to get worked up about the frightful things we'd seen and look on the bright side of life. My partner backed him up. After further influence had been brought to bear on Eva, whose nerves were shattered, she agreed to spend a few minutes in the table tennis room, whether in an active or passive capacity.

My partner went into the living room. There she placed the essentials (four glasses plus bottles of wine, beer, lemonade, cigarettes, lighter, ashtray, and chips) on the tray that had been used previously. With care, putting one foot slowly before the other, she carried everything up the steep stairs to the second floor.

Since my partner and Eva still had a few chores to do in the table tennis room (wiping the table in the corner, unloading the tray, shutting the windows, fetching cleaning rags or putting them away), Heinrich and I picked up the table tennis paddles. We started an informal rally without scoring. In the course of this, we remarked how refreshed we felt by this renewed opportunity to engage in physical activity. We struck the ball vigorously, heedless of the consequent fact that many of our shots missed and we had to go looking for it elsewhere in the room.

My partner drew our attention to the sound of the rain, which was no less thunderous than before. This led Heinrich to surmise that we were getting a whole month's rain in advance. Eva recalled a child's rhyme to the effect that the fourth month of the year is a law unto itself.

Heinrich exhorted the women to play, and we embarked on a mixed doubles. I once more found myself paired with Eva versus my partner and Heinrich. Eva is a good table tennis player, but her game displayed inaccuracies and even gross errors. Although he wasn't her partner, Heinrich reprimanded her for this. Eva flung her paddle down and went to sit in the corner at the card table, on which the drinks had been deposited. Looking tense, she informed us that she simply wasn't in the mood and couldn't do full justice to her talents, so we must finish the game on our own.

Heinrich said that two against one at table tennis was an unfair arrangement—unfair for the two. His efforts to persuade Eva to return bore no fruit, and an apology proved equally unsuccessful. With the score at 11:11, my partner announced that she too wanted to quit and would watch us—Heinrich and me—from the card table. Ignoring our protests, she sat down beside Eva. Heinrich and I had no choice but to play on by ourselves.

In a complete reversal of our normal relative strengths, I managed to win not only the first set but the second as well. This caused Heinrich to swear and eventually led him to accuse me of bewitching the ball and my opponent. His indignation attained such a pitch that it even sent Eva, who had been plunged in melancholy, into fits of laughter. Heinrich thereupon stepped up the frequency of his expletives so as to create a jocular, relaxed atmosphere. My partner stated that she had never thought Heinrich capable of pulling such silly faces. Her remark was likewise greeted with delight.

After I had won the third set as well (the first two had ended 21:19 and 21:17, respectively), Eva yawned and stretched, saying that she felt the need to go to bed. This intention was fiercely opposed by my partner. We saw each other too seldom because of the great distance between us, she argued, so it was wrong not to make the most of our time together.

Eva replied that she was exhausted and incapable of being congenial company, but she promised to fix us a first-class breakfast early the next morning and make herself available for a whole day's communal activities and entertainment thereafter. When my partner made another attempt to change her mind and broached the possibility of her drinking a martini, Eva vigorously shook her head.

She rose and wished us good night, though we ran into her again downstairs. This was because the three of us left in the game room had thought it advisable to return to the living room, where we planned to round off the evening with wine and conversation.

While Eva was brushing her teeth, she talked to Heinrich—hampered by the foam in her mouth and the motion of the toothbrush therein—about the duties incumbent upon him as host the next day (sweeping the floor and beating the carpets). Heinrich said she was out of her mind; those things could be done after their guests had left. We supported him in that view.

After Eva had retired, Heinrich, my partner, and I sat down in the living room. My partner had kindly carried the tray of drinks, etc., downstairs from the game room. She suggested playing a game of rummy, but her suggestion aroused no enthusiasm, nor did her wish to play a guessing game. In that case, she said disappointedly, she was going to the bathroom.

Once she had disappeared, Heinrich confided in a low voice that he wanted to see if the murder video program was over. He turned on the television and muted the sound at once. The screen was showing the woman presenter we'd seen before. Fine, said Heinrich, we could start watching at the earliest opportunity. He wound the tape back.

My partner still hadn't returned, so we agreed to start watching the video right away, though with the sound turned down so as not to disturb Eva's sleep.

At 1:35, the long-haired brother's face reappeared on the screen. He was still refusing to speak but was also prevented from doing so by the need to vomit. At 1:51, a barn came into view. We saw the two boys running toward it, the camera unsteadily keeping up with them.

At that moment, my partner came into the living room. She grasped the situation and scolded us. She didn't feel like watching this now, she said. Heinrich said he couldn't restrain his curiosity any longer. She would forgo the opportunity, she retorted, and wished us good night.

When the sound of her footsteps on the wooden stairs had died away, Heinrich asked me if she was offended. I responded—truthfully—with a shrug.

Smoke was just rising from the barn. The children emerged and paused beside the gate to watch the progress of their handiwork. When the whole building went up in flames at 2:03, Heinrich approvingly remarked that they were smart boys; it couldn't have been easy to torch a barn so quickly and effectively.

The boys were interviewed again, this time about their attitude to arson. Did they enjoy playing with fire? The cameraman received no satisfactory replies, so he asked if they would like to set fire to their brother's corpse. Did they know what burning flesh smelled like? Sobbing anew, they answered both questions in the negative.

Heinrich dug me in the ribs. Could I conceive of such a thing? he asked. Could I put myself in the cameraman's place? It defied one's comprehension. What could be going on inside such a person?

2:42. "Screening this video is not sensationalism. It is a vain attempt to come to terms with an incomprehensible human tragedy."

The long-haired brother was standing on the thickest root of a massive tree. He was enjoined to look at the camera with a cheerful expression. The cameraman said he was sure he wanted to leave behind a favorable impression of himself. If he were crying in the very last pictures of him, it would be bound to vex his mother. Contrary to instructions, the boy began to cry and, like his gap-toothed brother before him, hopped up and down on the spot.

The cameraman angrily complained that hopping up and down did not make a suitable contribution to a nice film, still less render it easier for his mother to take leave of a son. Couldn't he imagine how distressed she would be to see him like this? In floods of tears, the boy whimpered something unintelligible. The cameraman told him to enunciate more clearly.

The long-haired brother now said, audibly, that he didn't want to die and he possessed a savings book into which his grandmother had long been making regular payments. If he were released at once, he would let the cameraman have this savings book.

How did he propose to send it? he was asked.

He could, for instance, entrust it to the postal service, replied the anguished boy. The cameraman rejected this offer. Besides, he said, the savings book wasn't enough. Hadn't he anything more valuable? The long-haired brother talked of a money box. His parents sometimes put coins in it, and it hadn't been taken to the bank for months. It occurred to the hog-tied brother that he possessed a similar savings book. He also owned an expensive bicycle, which he would relinquish in the cameraman's favor. The latter replied that this was insufficient too, and ordered the long-haired brother to climb the tree. The response was a loud, protesting wail.

Heinrich, helping himself to a handful of chips, said, How frightful. That man must be the devil incarnate.

The camera showed the long-haired brother weeping and slobbering in close-up. The camera wobbled. The croaking voice bade the long-haired brother to look at the camera. If he continued to resist, the salting of the hog-tied brother's abdominal cavity would commence at once. Then it would be the rest of the family's turn. Reference was also made to the cameraman's knife.

Accompanied by outraged exclamations from Heinrich, the long-haired brother could be seen starting to climb the tree, still weeping and bawling at the top of his voice. How terrible, said Heinrich. What can be going through the boy's mind? Is he thinking the same as we would?

I asked what we would be thinking.

It's awful, he said; they ought to pass laws that could prevent such things.

I asked what he meant but was shushed in reply.

Now that the long-haired brother had taken up his position in the treetop, the cameraman proceeded to question the hog-tied boy. You're on television, my boy, he said. Kindly tell our viewers what you feel about the fact that your brother is about to jump off a tree.

Boohoo, the boy replied.

This is revolting, said Heinrich. He asked if I would object if he briefly freeze-framed the film because he proposed to get himself another portion of ice cream from the kitchen. Not at all, I said. He inquired if I would like some too. I thanked him but declined. I wasn't hungry and felt no desire for any ice cream. He retired to the kitchen, to return shortly afterward and deposit his bowl of ice cream on the table. Then he restarted the film.

The interview with the hog-tied boy wasn't over yet. He made another reference to his savings book. This prompted the cameraman to ask about his grandmother. Did she suffer from diabetes or heart disease, and didn't they, the two boys, consider it seemly to behave less hysterically? After all, these pictures might be made available to their grandmother and give her a heart attack. The cameraman wanted their grandmother to be able to say that the two boys had handled themselves well. He could picture the old woman sitting in front of the television. She would clasp her hands together and say, It had to be this way, but they both behaved well.

The camera voice called to the long-haired boy up the tree. It was time for him to put on a good show, it said. He should console himself with the thought that, by jumping, he was doing his surviving brother a favor. After all, the family would have far more money available for the hog-tied brother to spend on expensive bicycles and deposit in his savings book. That should surely gratify the occupant of the treetop?

The long-haired brother wept and shook his head.

The cameraman deplored this, saying that envy gets you nowhere in life. He announced that the boy would have to jump in precisely ten minutes. If he obeyed instructions, nothing would happen to anyone else in his family. But if he jumped even one second too late, the hog-tied brother's abdominal cavity would be slit open and filled with salt and red ants. After that, devastation would be visited on his parents' farmhouse. His mother would be boiled alive, his father slowly cut to ribbons, etc. His grandmother too would be run to earth, and old women burned nicely.

Heinrich observed that the man behind the camera must be thoroughly sick.

The long-haired brother made no reply, so the cameraman inquired what it felt like, the prospect of dying in eight minutes forty seconds' time. The boy shouted something unintelligible in a voice rendered hoarse by his previous bawling, yelling, and vomiting. Then he fell silent and stared into space.

Fancy, said Heinrich, he's on another planet.

The cameraman turned to the hog-tied boy. Was it a nice feeling, owing his life to his own brother's death? The boy thus addressed denied this. Or would he rather change places with him? he was asked. The boy beneath the tree stopped crying and stared fixedly at the camera. The cameraman repeated that he could save the other boy's life by taking his place. The hog-tied brother yelled something unintelligible, and more whimpering could be heard from overhead.

Cut. 3:20. The cameraman reiterated all his threats to the long-haired brother in the event that he failed to jump in fifty seconds' time. One second later, and everyone would meet a terrible end. Screams from up the tree.

Heinrich, who described them as bloodcurdling, felt compelled to wipe his eyes on the back of his hand.

There was still time, the cameraman told the hog-tied boy. He had thirty-five seconds in which to decide to take his brother's place and dive off the tree headfirst, the way he did into the swimming pool in summer. The boy stared at the camera, weeping but bereft of speech.

Another twenty seconds, said the voice.

A family appeared: father, mother, and two children. The parents were discussing financial investments. Heinrich sighed and said, Here we go again. As before, we were accorded some ten minutes in which to devote ourselves to conversation, or chips and suchlike, before the forest reappeared.

Another twenty seconds, said the voice. Then the hog-tied brother took a step forward and went out of shot. The camera panned down. The boy could be seen clutching the cameraman's leg and imploring him not to make anyone jump at all. The voice called a warning and started to count: five, four, three, two, one...

We heard a scream but could see only a black screen. The channel had evidently censored this scene as well. The ticker repeated that screening this video was not sensationalism, but a vain attempt to come to terms with an incomprehensible human tragedy. Counselors' phone numbers were inserted, together with the note to the effect that callers would be charged only a maximum of €0.50 per minute.

The forest reappeared, and we heard the tearful voice of the hog-tied brother. The sound abruptly ceased and the screen went black.

Outside the house, rain was beating down with undiminished intensity.

Heinrich laid the remote control aside. He'd had enough, he said; he didn't want to see any more. How sick and degenerate the people who watched so-called snuff movies must be.

I pointed out that the third brother's escape was also bound to be shown and was still to come, so that might cheer him up. Heinrich replied that he would watch it tomorrow; he wanted to check the Internet to see if the killer had been caught or if the police at least had a lead.

"West Styria: Police net tightens. Checks have been run on dozens of people in the course of the hunt for the killer. Little information has emanated from the Ministry of the Interior because of the news blackout, but it is rumored that the killer has not yet left the area or may be a local inhabitant."

Heinrich loudly demanded how they knew this.

"Violent protests against the transmission of the murder video. The German commercial station that transmitted parts of the so-called murder video during the night has been very sharply criticized by all schools of thought at home and abroad. The German president has called it a disgrace to the whole of Germany and publicly apologized to his Austrian colleagues. He referred to a failure of media policy and said he saw evidence of moral decay. One recourse might be stricter media legislation."

Stupid idiots, said Heinrich.

Eva entered in her nightgown. She said hello and sat down on the arm of the sofa, which consisted of a white bolster. Heinrich stroked her back and solicitously inquired why she couldn't sleep. He picked up some chips and put them in his mouth. Chewing noisily, he jerked his thumb at the window and said it would soon be light. Eva disputed this, saying there were still a couple of hours to go.

I went into the bathroom, where I washed my face with soap, brushed my teeth, and dried myself on one of Heinrich and Eva's hand towels, which was adorned with a smiling cartoon character named the Pink Panther.

I returned to the living room. Eva was just taking her leave. She asked when Heinrich was thinking of following her up to bed. Soon, he replied. She waved to us and left the room.

Heinrich offered me some chips. I helped myself. He poured himself some red wine from a dark-green, opaque bottle, sighed, and read some more news.

I was so tired I stretched out in my armchair and briefly closed my eyes. When I awoke, the sun was shining outside. The time by the video recorder was 8:18. Heinrich was lying asleep on the sofa with his mouth open.

I heard Eva's voice outside the door. Those two idiots spent the night in the living room, she was saying. Then my partner made herself heard. She indignantly conjectured that the two "weary warriors" wouldn't be much use to anyone today.

I raised my head and looked at the door.

Aha, said Eva, one of them is awake.

My partner tapped her forehead at me. I wished her good morning. In consequence of our brief ensuing conversation, Heinrich woke up too. He jumped to his feet as though someone had tipped a bucket of cold water over him. He just took the time to give his wife a good-morning kiss as he brushed past her.

I rubbed my eyes and plodded out into the hall to join the others.

Heinrich slipped into his brown sandals and asked where the car keys were. Hanging on their hook as usual, said Eva, but what did he need the car for? Heinrich replied that he had to buy some newspapers. Eva said he was mad; he ought to have some breakfast first, and besides, there probably weren't any papers on Easter Sunday. Heinrich recalled the *Kronen Zeitung*'s advertisement of last night, which had promised to bring out an edition containing an illustrated sixteen-page report on the killings.

He was almost out the door when, with his sunglasses on his nose, he hurried back into the living room and turned on the television, exclaiming that they might have caught him.

The news reported that a hectic manhunt was in progress. The killer's trail had been picked up. Having feverishly zapped from channel to channel, Heinrich tossed the remote control onto the sofa and stormed out. Soon afterward, we heard the car start up. The sound of the engine receded.

Eva and my partner set about making breakfast. My help was not, in their opinion, necessary, so I returned to the living room and sat down in the armchair in which I had involuntarily spent the night. I thoroughly perused the news online, which I had only been able to skim, thanks to Heinrich's hurried mode of procedure.

Under "Riots outside TV station": The station that transmitted the so-called murder video was besieged during the night by demonstrators, of whom some unidentified late-stayers attacked the building with paint bombs at around 4:30 a.m.

Under "Vigil in West Styrian town": In Frauenkirchen, even on such a stormy, rainy night, hundreds of people kept a vigil in the street. Indignation was aroused by a report that the perpetrator might be a local inhabitant. This was inconceivable, said the mayor. The killer was a person of unprecedented brutality, and no such individual lived in this district.

Under "Criticism of Referendum Plan": Violent reactions have been provoked by the Freedom Party's consideration of whether to petition for a referendum on the reintroduction of the death penalty. The parliamentary speaker declares that this would place Austria outside the European community of values.

I returned to the kitchen. Eva was humming a tune as she poured boiling water into a pot, disseminating an aroma of coffee. My partner handed me a tablecloth.

I went out into the paved drive in the front yard. It was exceptionally warm for the time of day. I had to shoo four cats off the table before I could spread the cloth, though my approach and my gesticulations proved sufficient for the purpose. That done, I noticed there were some bird droppings adhering to the table. Although my intention had been to spread the cloth over the table, I fetched a swab from the house to wipe it first. Only then did I complete my task.

I sat down on one of the wooden benches that had been placed on either side of the massive table. For around ten minutes, I watched the activities of the cats, approximately twenty of which had reappeared. Some frolicked with each other, others lay around in idleness. I also saw the fancy-dress cat I had encountered in the loft during the night. I wondered whether it was sweating inside its garments or suffering in some other manner.

Meanwhile, my partner and Eva brought out plates, cutlery, glasses, bottles, napkins, bread baskets, bottled preserves, saltcellar and pepper pot, butter, jam, plates of cheese, sausage, milk, sugar, and last of all, the coffeepot. When my partner caught sight of the dressed-up cat, she burst out laughing and said she'd never seen anything so absurd.

We decided not to wait for Heinrich any longer. Eva said it was silly of him to go gallivanting around in the car, and it was his own fault if he turned up too late for breakfast.

The farmer emerged from the house next door. This morning too he was wearing his undersized hat and a jacket unsuited to the high prevailing temperature. Eva expressed the hope that he wouldn't join us; he would be bound to talk about the killings and make her feel uneasy. The farmer waved. In his wontedly stolid manner, he plodded over to the stables, in which sundry animals were making themselves heard.

My partner poured some coffee. She bit into an open sausage sandwich and looked up at the sun. Masticating, she said it was a glorious day and it mustn't be spoiled by talk of murder and so on; Eva should bring influence to bear on Heinrich in that regard. She wouldn't forgive me either if I dared to disturb this idyllic day of rest.

While conversing about the length of time the Stubenrauchs had lived there, what the infrastructure was like (doctors, shops, gas stations), and how much of every day Eva and Heinrich devoted to driving to their respective places of work, we tucked into our breakfast. After a while, we were obliged to put up the sun umbrella. The butter on the table had nearly melted and the milk was threatening to turn sour. Because I was seated nearest the jam jar, it fell to me to shoo away ten wasps or so.

Just as the farmer emerged from the stables, the Stubenrauchs' car drove into the yard. Heinrich got out with a bundle of newspapers under his arm. The farmer came over to us. He said good morning, more to Heinrich than the rest of us. Heinrich only just had time to nod to us before the farmer, in his usual, overly loud way of speaking, launched into a conversation about the murders. Eva and my partner reacted with unconcealed displeasure, but Heinrich promptly seized on the farmer's assertion that the killer couldn't be a local and that such a thing was out of the question.

While driving, said Heinrich, he had read in the paper that the police were looking for a red sedan of Japanese manufacture with old Styrian license plates. Eva took him to task. He was mad to read while driving, she told him. With a grin, Heinrich pointed out that nothing untoward had happened.

The farmer said that, although he might believe the bit about the Styrian license plates, the murderer certainly wasn't from the neighborhood; there were no such persons anywhere in the locality.

Depositing the newspapers on the table, Heinrich retorted that one couldn't see inside people's heads.

I opened one of the papers. It featured a big picture of a boy pointing with an outstretched arm to a spot at the top of a tree. A black, downward-pointing arrow had been drawn from that spot to indicate the jumping-off point, the victim's trajectory, and his point of impact. My partner, who had initially averted her gaze, leaned over and asked if that was the surviving child.

No, I said, it was a faked photograph; the tree was authentic but not the boy.

Incredible, that tree, said the farmer. He knew the forest, it was a good place for picking mushrooms, he'd been there more than once but had never guessed that something so terrible would happen there someday—how could he? The killer must be found at all costs and made short work of. So saying, he turned and ambled back to his house.

Heinrich sat down at the table at last. Hurriedly, he poured himself a cup of coffee, then took a bite out of a dry roll and immersed himself in a newspaper. Wouldn't he at least put some butter on it? Eva demanded. Heinrich merely grunted, said Hmm, and remained totally incommunicado.

She said he should restrain himself. He mustn't forget that their guests hadn't made the long journey to Styria just to watch television and read newspapers. This was a day for relaxation and amicable conversation, she said, so put the paper away.

Heinrich laughed and did as he was told, but he said he couldn't detach himself from the tragedy completely. He had at least to keep abreast of events during the day or his curiosity would choke him. Eva and my partner rolled their eyes but conceded this, whereupon he jumped up and hurried into the house. She hadn't meant it that way, Eva called after him, but he had disappeared.

Pretexting a visit to the bathroom, I likewise went inside, pursued by the women's cries of disapproval. Heinrich, with a newspaper open on his knees, was seated in front of the television perusing the news. In a conspiratorial tone of voice, he said he was acquainted with a policeman who performed his duties in Frauenkirchen. He felt strongly tempted to call him, or even to pay him a visit; we might be able to glean some information that hadn't been publicized by the newspapers or on television.

I reminded him that such a course of action would inevitably result in protests from the female members of our foursome. Shaking his head, Heinrich said they must be given some incentive for taking an equal interest in the progress of the case. When I inquired about the nature of this incentive, he replied in one word: Fear.

It would be reprehensible of us, he said with a grin, but we could at least inspire a certain uneasiness, for instance by reporting rumors that the killer was on the loose somewhere nearby; I need only remember the fuss they had made last night. No, he added, it really wasn't necessary to scare our womenfolk stiff. If we were clever, we could use pure conjecture to persuade them not to put too much of a brake on our research.

We re-devoted ourselves to the news and the newspaper, respectively. The paper described the killer as an inhuman, bestial, camera-wielding devil, a criminal from another planet. His atrocities were the focus of every columnist and commentator. Even a picture of the victims' mother had been printed. The article informed us that this photograph was considered scandalous. The photographer had sneaked into the Am Feldhof psychiatric institute disguised as a nurse and photographed the murdered boys' mother, who was strapped to a bed and internally suffused with medication. According to the article, the chairman of the Press Council and the leader of the Liberal Party had stated that this conflicted with their ethical principles.

After Heinrich and I had read each other some interesting excerpts from various newspaper columns, we went outside again. The women greeted us with sullen faces and reproachful expressions. Heinrich ignored them.

Excitedly, he announced that the killer had been identified but the police were still unwilling to reveal who he was. Did that mean they had caught him? Eva demanded. Heinrich said no, but they thought they knew roughly where he was—namely, in this area. He had been sighted on Rössel Road between Frauenkirchen and Kaibing.

My partner agitatedly inquired the source of this information. Heinrich said we had heard it on the radio. My partner sprang to her feet, as did Eva, and hurried into the house. She turned on the radio and asked which station had broadcast the news. Austria 2, the local Styrian station, Heinrich replied. My partner tuned the radio on, but in order to receive the station she had to change frequencies. This aroused her suspicions.

Heinrich hastened to reassure her; in search of further information, he had gone looking for another station. Then my partner found Austria 2. Blaring folk music could be heard. Startled, she turned the sound down. Eva had joined us by now.

Heinrich urged the two of them not to be concerned—nor to make such a spectacle of themselves as they had last night after the din in the loft. My partner irritably retorted that they hadn't made a spectacle of themselves and that the camera killer's potential proximity genuinely alarmed her. Heinrich replied that the killer had every reason to be more frightened of us and everyone else than we were of him. Yes, Eva added, and it was broad daylight now too.

So no one need be frightened, said Heinrich, and a good thing too.

Eva said she must nip over to the farmer to fetch some milk fresh from the cow. My partner volunteered to accompany her, saying that it was a long time since she'd seen such a thing. Eva said she wouldn't actually be milking the cow—the milk came from a churn—but my partner insisted that this, combined with the smell of stables, would give her equal pleasure.

Once the two of them had left the house, Heinrich beckoned to me and hurried into the living room. He wanted to watch the end of the video, he said; he was feeling full of beans and less squeamish today, and he hoped the killer would soon be caught. So saying, he turned on the television and the video recorder.

3:59. The cameraman was interviewing the hog-tied brother about the emotions that had beset him since his brother's death. When he received no satisfactory answers, he reminded the boy that he could have saved his brother's life. Tears were the sole response.

The cameraman then told him that he at least had an opportunity to save his mother from being boiled alive and his father from being dismembered. He, the cameraman, would shut his eyes and count to a hundred. It was up to the boy whether he remained where he was or ran off. If he stayed, he would be put to death in the most painless manner possible and his entire family, grandmother included, would be spared. If he ran away, he would be pursued. If the cameraman failed to catch him at once or within the next few hours, he would pay the family a visit on October 31st and Halloween them all to death. The police would be powerless to help. If he caught the boy at once, however, he would kill him after salting his abdominal cavity, making a necktie out of his tongue, and scrambling his innards from behind, etc. He would also murder one other member of the family— either mother, father, or grandmother—with the aid of various implements such as pliers and scissors, etc., but spare the rest and leave the choice of the victim to the boy. He was telling him this to give him a chance to come to his senses; in the event that he ran away, he could turn around and at least save two members of his family.

Heinrich said he'd never encountered such a person in his life, and he regretted not being one of the policemen actively involved in hunting for the killer; he would gladly exchange a few words with the fellow.

The cameraman said he would now start counting. Cut. 4:09. The camera panned across the whole terrain. Not a child in sight anywhere.

The presenter reappeared on screen. She urgently advised viewers to use the TV station's psychological counseling service. Telephone numbers were screened.

Heinrich switched off. Now we know, he said. He hoped the women would soon be back with the milk; he wanted to drive to Frauenkirchen and try to make contact with his acquaintance in the police.

Since the women still hadn't returned, he offered to play a game of sixty-six with me. He went and got the deck of cards. I won the first game. Halfway through the second, the score stood at 4:3 to Heinrich.

Just then, the women came in. They expressed surprise that we weren't sitting in front of the television, studying the latest reports. Eva said they had paid a brief visit to the farmer and his wife. Sadly, not a normal word had been uttered; the house next door was dominated by the murders. The farmer's wife had been sitting in the kitchen in tears. Terribly upset by her crying fit, the farmer had stomped around and announced his intention of fetching his rifle. Eva had injudiciously mentioned Heinrich's Austria 2 report to the effect that the killer was heading in our direction. The farmer had promptly proceeded to put his threat into effect and made to leave the kitchen to get his gun. A dramatic scene ensued.

The farmer's wife barred his exit from the kitchen and loudly implored him not to bring misfortune down on their heads. She argued that a certain Alois Schober, who turned out to be a policeman known to the farmer's family, would clinch matters either on his own or with his colleagues. The farmer ordered her to get out of his way. He didn't intend to join the manhunt, he said; he merely planned to defend his farm if the murderer showed up there; were he to put a bullet in the scoundrel's head, it would be an accident or self-defense or both. Eva too endeavored to calm the farmer down but was flatly ignored by him.

Heinrich asked how the incident had ended. The farmer's wife was sitting distraught in the kitchen, said Eva, and the farmer was probably loading his rifle. Laughing, Heinrich expressed the theory that we truly weren't safe here anymore—not because of the murderer, whose advent was unlikely, but because of a neighbor who was not only armed but obviously overwrought. My partner said she didn't think this funny. Heinrich pooh-poohed her interjection and said the farmer would simmer down.

If the ladies insisted on doing something today, he suggested driving to Frauenkirchen, where he wanted to try to locate the policeman of his acquaintance.

What policeman? asked Eva.

The one who had been so helpful and informative when he was changing his car papers, Heinrich replied. He'd told her about him—surely she must remember?

Actually, said my partner, she'd had something different in mind.

Eva sighed. The murderer had completely ruined her weekend, she said, but in view of the existence of the Café Wurm, she would consent to go to Frauenkirchen. My partner reminded Eva that some people's weekend had been even more thoroughly ruined than hers.

Heinrich nodded, raised his arms, and flapped them like a child falling from a great height. My partner called him a monster. Eva said she was well acquainted with his obnoxious and incurable cynicism. Heinrich laughed and said sorry, he couldn't help himself; his gesture had been prompted by an inner compulsion. The women shook their heads.

Eva said that any repetition of such behavior would cause her to obey an inner compulsion to slap his face.

Well, said Heinrich, how about it? Were they coming, or was he to drive to Frauenkirchen on his own?

My partner retorted that he was out of his mind. She wouldn't stay here on her own for anything in the world, not with a trigger-happy farmer twenty yards away and the prospect of encountering the camera killer.

Eva said that going to Frauenkirchen presented an opportunity to partake of an iced coffee at the Café Wurm. In the meantime, those two (meaning Heinrich and me) could go in search of their policeman.

Fine, said my partner, she liked iced coffee; above all, though, she would feel safer with other people around.

Heinrich clapped his hands and said, Let's go.

My partner and Eva protested that they hadn't changed or made their faces up. That could take some time, Heinrich groaned, and he invited me to resume our card game. I declined because it occurred to me that I still hadn't brushed my teeth that morning. I wanted to remedy this deficiency and have a shower as well. Heinrich brusquely said there really wasn't time for that, so I agreed to temporarily confine myself to brushing my teeth and washing my face and make up for the omission by showering that afternoon.

Heinrich: You don't imagine I've had a wash, do you? Eva overheard this and called him a pig. He chuckled but accompanied me into the bathroom, where we attended to our dental hygiene, standing side by side at the sink.

Eva laughed. Summoning my partner, she pointed to us and said, Didn't we look sweet, like a brace of oxen in a stable.

Heinrich splashed the womenfolk with water and they withdrew.

When we were through, we went outside and took up our positions by the car. Its bodywork, which had been considerably heated by the sun, precluded any physical contact with it. We passed the time in trivial conversation. Now and then Heinrich would call in the direction of the house, demanding to know when the ladies might be expected to put in an appearance.

We chatted about the exceptional number of cats that were once more populating the yard, their problems in finding or obtaining food, and whether it mightn't be better to castrate or sterilize them. Heinrich said the farmer was loath to spend any money on this but had devised a birth-control program of his own. Whenever a female turned up with her litter, he took the kittens away from their mother and flung them at a tree as hard as he could, killing them. This was undoubtedly cruel, but (a) it was the custom around here, and (b) the mother cats had become smart enough to conceal their offspring from the farmer and his attentions until they were big enough to fend for themselves. The farmer's wife had told him all this one Sunday four weeks ago, Heinrich said in conclusion.

My partner and Eva appeared at last. Heinrich opened the door for them. My partner said we could be sure she wouldn't be first to enter the house on our return. Even Eva grinned at this.

We got into the Stubenrauchs' car. Heinrich seated himself at the wheel with me in the passenger seat and Eva and my partner behind us on the left and right, respectively. When driving out, we had to be careful not to run over any cats, but the animals were well trained and fled in all directions when the car started up. Heinrich said one could never tell.

When we were out on the highway, he suggested making a deal with the farmer: The latter should undertake to pay him a certain sum or give him a rebate on his monthly rent for every cat he killed. He was sure the man would agree, he said. Eva told him to stop it. Heinrich added that the deal was impracticable, in any case, because the task of washing feline remains off his tires would be too distasteful. Eva asked why he always had to rile her in such a disgusting manner. Heinrich laughed and promised to say no more.

He turned on the radio. According to the news, the German commercial station that transmitted the murder video had laid itself open to penalties ranging from a substantial fine to withdrawal of its broadcasting license. Heinrich said that things were never as black as they were painted; he felt sure the broadcasters had sufficient contacts with politicians and other influential individuals to stave off the worst. My partner agreed. Those people knew the ropes, she said.

Referring to the manhunt, the newscaster stated that several leads to the murderer's car had been followed up, but also to actual persons, all of them residents in West Styria, and that investigations were in full swing. Heinrich said he very much hoped his policeman acquaintance would be able to provide more details.

Eva started to talk to my partner about iced coffee and the Café Wurm. The ice creams there were of the highest quality, she said, and the cakes weren't to be sneezed at either. My partner inquired whether the Café Wurm stocked Malakoff tortes. Eva said she didn't know, but its range of cakes and pastries was so large that the chances were very good.

The radio announcer said they would shortly be broadcasting a sound excerpt from the murder video in order to publicize the killer's voice. Oh no, said Eva, and my partner exclaimed that she didn't need this. Eva leaned forward between the front seats and urgently requested Heinrich to change stations at once. He shrugged and inserted a cassette in the deck. Eva sat back again and said, Thanks very much.

After a while, my partner asked Heinrich to drive somewhat slower and refrain from cornering so sharply because she was starting to feel sick. Heinrich claimed to be driving as sedately as an angel, but he moderated his speed for the rest of the trip.

On arrival in Frauenkirchen, we soon had to leave the car behind. There was no hope of finding a parking place in the middle of town, so we got out and proceeded on foot. On the way, we saw cars and buses bearing inscriptions that betrayed they belonged to broadcasting personnel.

Orally and by pointing, Eva drew our attention to the local church, which was draped in black bunting. A lot of the houses too were flying black flags. On closer inspection, many of these turned out to be skirts, pants, coats, blankets, etc.

The end justifies the means, said Heinrich.

It's the gesture that counts, Eva added.

My partner said she couldn't believe how crowded the town was and could already sense the dismal atmosphere prevailing there. She had underestimated this and doubted her ability to relish any Malakoff torte.

Meantime, Heinrich had broken into a trot and was some thirty feet ahead of us. I increased my own rate of advance. When I caught up to him, he called over his shoulder that he and I would go to the police station; Eva and my partner should go to the Café Wurm, and we would join them there later.

Heinrich towed me across the street by my shirtsleeve. There was such a crush we had difficulty making any progress, and I had to be careful not to lose him in the crowd.

Near the church, we encountered the Easter procession, which was evidently on its way back from the cemetery after collecting the body of Our Lord. In the lead were three ministrants with a cross. Behind them came the parish priest flanked by schoolchildren and altar boys bearing holy water, and ordinary worshipers brought up the rear.

Here comes Christ's mortician, quipped Heinrich.

The people around us removed their headgear. There was little talking. Spectators who were obviously from out of town stared at the procession and conversed in low voices. It took us considerable time to get anywhere near the police station. Unoccupied patrol cars were parked there with their blue lights flashing. They were cordoned off from the crowd by ropes and policemen armed with radios and pistols, presumably to enable the vehicles to enter and leave.

Here we are, said Heinrich, but how do we get in? In fact, we were unable even to reach the rope across the entrance to the police station. This is ridiculous, said Heinrich. He thought for a moment, then said he would phone; it must be possible to telephone the station—someone might want to report an emergency.

And so, grunting and mopping our perspiring brows, we made our way to back to a bus stop, beside which, in addition to the bus shelter, stood a public telephone booth. Heinrich had no small change. I felt in my pocket and handed him two twenty-cent coins and six ten-cent pieces. He asked me to wait outside the booth, saying that it was too cramped to accommodate us both. Besides, the heat would render a sojourn inside it even more unpleasant for a twosome, and anyway, he didn't care to be listened to when he was on the phone.

In the course of the approximately fifteen minutes I spent standing around idly outside the booth, two people, clearly local inhabitants, came up and handed me a sheet of yellow paper. It bore an artist's impression of the killer and a description of his clothing. Beneath this were telephone numbers to be called for the purpose of passing on relevant information. Right at the foot, someone had added by hand: *Reward €10,000 (Herr Josef Federl of Federl's Mill)*. The whole thing was ill-printed and askew, and the sheet was dog-eared.

Heinrich emerged from the telephone booth. Peering over my shoulder, he remarked that the picture bore a resemblance not only to his mother-in-law but to one of the stray cats in the farmyard.

I asked him what he had managed to glean. Nothing, he said, though not for want of trying more than once. The friendly policeman hadn't been at all friendly today; he had said he responded to emergency calls only and would not divulge any information. Heinrich had called again, this time pretending to be a journalist, but had been advised to attend the forthcoming press conference.

We betook ourselves to the Café Wurm, surveyed the tables in the garden without sighting our womenfolk, and went inside. The establishment was grossly overcrowded. Waitresses in white aprons were threading their way through the throng of standing or seated customers with trays above their heads. Although every window and door was wide open, the place was thick with tobacco smoke.

Someone tapped me on the shoulder. It was my partner. She said we must be blind; she and Eva had been sitting in the garden and had waved to us. We followed her outside. There was one chair too few, but Heinrich soon managed to get hold of another. I noticed that lying on every table was a yellow leaflet like the one I'd been handed outside the telephone booth.

We ordered coffees. Heinrich reported on his fruitless endeavors.

My partner, who said she found the café thoroughly uncongenial, urged us to drink up.

Eva asked Heinrich what was so interesting about the next table, and why he had to stare at it with his back to us. He replied that seated there was the deputy mayor, the local police chief's best friend, who was outlining the situation with the aid of a map. Without a by-your-leave, he pulled up his chair to the next table and asked exactly where the killer was being sought. So as not to miss anything, I went and stood behind him.

When the deputy mayor took a pencil and proceeded to draw on the map, even my partner and Eva rose from their chairs—the cushions were covered in some cheap, pink-floral material—and came to watch.

The deputy mayor said, "There, you see? That's where we're looking. The whole area is cordoned off, and we're closing in."

Heinrich asked if that meant they had a suspect who was presumed to be inside the circle he'd drawn.

"Yes," the deputy mayor replied, "that's right."

Eva exclaimed that her home was plumb in the middle of that circle, and she didn't like the sound of it at all.

My partner called for the check. The waitress, who happened to be serving a table nearby, took a big, black wallet from her apron. My partner inquired whether the Stubenrauchs would mind if we invited them to lunch at an inn. We had given them a great deal of work this weekend, she said, and would like to show our appreciation. Eva dismissed this proposal. My partner pointed out that we would have to eat anyway and that preparing a meal (cooking) would take up a lot of time that could be put to better use.

Eva looked at Heinrich, who said we could certainly eat out, but there was no question of our inviting them; they would invite us, being their guests. My partner and I fiercely disputed this, and we eventually prevailed on the Stubenrauchs to let us play host. Heinrich said he knew of a fairly secluded inn about half-way between Frauenkirchen and their house—one that ought to be unaffected by the turbulence prevailing in the victims' hometown. My partner welcomed this suggestion, and we walked back to the car.

On the way, Heinrich pointed out with a touch of pride that his good relations with a local bigwig (the deputy mayor) had secured us some important information about the manhunt. Eva said he was a hell of a fellow, and we all chuckled.

As soon as we had taken our places in the car and fastened our safety belts, we wound the side windows down because the heat inside the car generated by continuous solar radiation far exceeded the limits of what was tolerable.

Heinrich chauffeured us to the inn of his choice without occasioning my partner any further discomfort.

The parking lot was choked with cars. Whew, said my partner, it's a popular place. Since two more cars had pulled up behind us and their occupants were getting out, we hurried to the terrace of the inn for fear of losing a vacant table to people who had gotten there after us. There were no free tables at all, however. Eva suggested going in search of another inn. Heinrich swore that his hunger had attained an intensity that precluded another change of location, so we sat down inside the restaurant. My partner expressed her satisfaction that the windows, at least, were open, which created a pleasant through draft.

A loud, monotonous voice was issuing from an adjacent room. Heinrich went to investigate. Returning, he reported that the pope was on television. He was delivering his *Urbi et Orbi* while the occupants of the next room slurped their food and crossed themselves.

After we had ordered (four clear soups with strips of pancake, beef goulash for Heinrich, grilled Swiss for Eva, veal escalope with cream for my partner, and egg dumplings for me, plus four mixed salads with pumpkinseed oil), my partner confessed to feeling uneasy about the thought of returning to the Stubenrauchs' house after the meal; the circle the deputy mayor had drawn had made her nervous. Heinrich: Didn't she realize that, if the killer was suspected of being there, the place would be swarming with police?

Eva endorsed this view; she also felt uneasy, she said, but we could rely on the forces of law and order.

During the meal, Eva skillfully contrived to speak of general topics (our jobs, our next vacation, visits to the dentist, a Spanish course at the adult education center), and the conversation that developed was lively and varied. It was 12:31 when Eva finished her meal—the last of us to do so. Heinrich mooted the possibility of ordering a dessert.

Before we could debate this question, something out of the ordinary occurred in the adjoining room. A commotion broke out. The waitresses stopped work and everyone crowded next door. Heinrich had just stood up for a better look when a loud, agitated voice suddenly rang out. Accompanied by the *flap-flap-flap* of a helicopter, it was clearly issuing from a television set. Heinrich beckoned and called to us to come at once. In company with the last people to leave their tables, we streamed into the room next door, which was now jam-packed.

Straight ahead, standing on top of a tall closet, was a big television set of approximately fifteen years' vintage. It was showing a view of some countryside taken from a helicopter (the sound and speed of travel made it unlikely that it was an ordinary airplane). People in the room were calling out place names they recognized. In a voice breaking with emotion, the reporter stated that the red VW Golf now being pursued by police cars belonged to a man suspected of being the camera killer, who was trying to evade arrest. "Perhaps, ladies and gentlemen, we shall very soon witness the capture of the world's vilest criminal—let us hope so. The whole country, nay, half of the world, is behind the brave men in uniform who are even now risking their lives at 100 mph on this road in West Styria."

Everyone in the room was yelling wildly: "They've nabbed the swine," "The bastard's going to be caught," "String him up," etc. The reporter referred to a roadblock that came into view soon afterward.

This is incredible, Heinrich shouted, just look.

And my partner pinched me on the arm.

A man beside me—someone I'd never seen before—turned to me and said they ought to shoot the camera killer on the spot, not let him get out of the car. A few bullets through the driver's door and he would have had it. Self-defense—something had glinted inside the car and they'd thought it was a gun. Bang-bang—simple as that. He toasted me with his beer mug.

The fugitive's car came to a stop with squad cars behind and beside it. Uproar in the room. One or two more thoughtful souls called for quiet.

The policemen jumped out of their cars and aimed their weapons at the figure seated in the sedan. After a while, the man got out with his hands up. Just as he was being handcuffed, the camera zoomed in as close as possible to the scene of the action. We could almost distinguish the man's features. The angry yelling in the inn reached its climax. After some minutes' noisy expressions of satisfaction, the helicopter reporter could be heard once more.

A little while later, a police chief appeared on the screen. He was asked by jostling, shoving journalists if that was the murderer. Had he been caught? The police chief replied that the young man was only one suspect among several. He had rendered himself exceptionally suspicious by dropping out of sight on the night of Holy Thursday, and the police had finally run him to earth at a remote country inn. All further questions would be answered at a press conference scheduled for 3:00 p.m.

At that moment, the proprietress turned off the television and called to everyone to go on with their meals. This injunction was greeted with universal hilarity. The crowd gradually dispersed.

As my partner and I slowly returned to our table, step by step, we were engaged in conversation by total strangers. Was he from around here? Had he murdered more than once? Shouldn't he have been killed on the spot? Would we take part in the referendum? And so on.

Back at the table, Heinrich said it was great. Yesterday they'd televised the service in St. Stephen's Cathedral, but today they'd cut off the pope in mid-benediction. The seculars had obviously won the power struggle at Austrian Broadcasting.

Eva cast her eyes up to heaven. She said she was very happy at the outcome of this business and trusted that all future conversations and their guests' last day (i.e., tomorrow) would be unspoiled by the subject of murder. My partner fervently agreed.

Heinrich, extracting a toothpick from its wrapper, which bore the printed inscription *Holz-Berger*, said he wasn't sure they'd gotten the right man. Eva rolled her eyes again and told him to stop it; he would find out soon enough.

Heinrich grinned and asked my partner if she was now prepared to be the first to enter the Stubenrauchs' house, possibly even on her own, and check it for the presence of some stranger who might be equipped with a video camera. Eva vigorously reprimanded him. It was time he stopped these silly games, she said; the matter was settled. Heinrich gleefully apologized. My partner brushed this aside. She wasn't going to drive herself insane anymore and was quite prepared to enter the house on her own.

Grinning, Heinrich told me in an undertone, but loudly enough for the others to hear, that the threat of the camera killer might have been dispelled, but there was still the maddened farmer roaming the countryside with his rifle and firing at anything that moved. This remark was greeted with amusement.

My partner asked for the check and I got out my wallet. The proprietress took the money in person. While doing so, she struck up a conversation about the captured murderer. It was awful, she said; they had just announced that he was a twenty-four-year-old from the locality—the cook had heard it on the radio in the kitchen. Heinrich asked if there was any doubt about the young man's guilt. The proprietress shrugged her shoulders, which were swathed in a black silk shawl adorned with a floral pattern, and said they wouldn't have arrested him otherwise.

My partner praised the quality of the dishes we had consumed and inquired if the restaurant used organically grown meat and vegetables. This the proprietress confirmed, substantiating her assurance by citing various names that meant nothing to us (Herbert Stadler, possibly a farmer, and Karl Gnam, a butcher). My partner commended this policy, and the proprietress regarded her with approval from then on. One could see and hear that my partner was a townswoman, she said, and city folk sometimes failed to appreciate natural products, though this situation was improving.

Last of all, she turned to the Stubenrauchs. She knew of them, she said, and they were well spoken of even though they hadn't lived in the district for long. Heinrich said he was interested to hear that; he'd had no idea they were a topic of conversation. Well, yes, said the proprietress, you know how people talk. The Stubenrauchs fitted in well locally, she went on. Johann Fleck, the mayor, with whom she was sure they were already acquainted, was someone you could always turn to in an emergency.

Heinrich laughed. If the camera killer showed up at their home, he said, he would be sure to notify Herr Fleck. Eva punched him in the ribs.

They've caught him anyway, the proprietress muttered.

Once my partner had finished her drink, we left the inn accompanied by good-byes all around. Several well-dressed children with smart haircuts were playing in the parking lot. Heinrich, who had gone on ahead, flapped his arms again. This resulted in a temperamental outburst on Eva's part. She declared that she wouldn't stand for any more of his cynicism. My partner backed her up. Eva said she meant it, and he should think before he spoke; he had made her look a fool at the inn with his talk of notifying the mayor about the murderer. Heinrich laughingly put his hands above his head as if defending himself from an assailant. Eva again said she meant it.

We got into the car. Heinrich was once more seated at the wheel with me in the passenger seat and the womenfolk accommodated in the back. Heinrich drove off. He said he proposed to make a short detour to enable us—meaning my partner and me—to savor the beauties of the surrounding countryside. He apologized for flapping his arms. Perhaps it was his way of coming to terms with what he'd seen, heard, and experienced. He was no psychologist, but he knew that many people dealt with such matters contemplatively, whereas others, of whom he was clearly one, adopted an aggressive approach. From behind us, Eva called out that this aggressive approach contained the seeds of another problem—namely, the danger of hurting the feelings of other, less coarse-grained individuals.

Heinrich said he was aware of this and apologized yet again; he would try to behave more acceptably in the future. He turned on the radio. Various people from the victims' hometown were being interviewed, among them someone who claimed to know the person who had been captured in the course of the manhunt. The man under arrest certainly wasn't the guilty party, he said; that was out of the question. All else apart, he had no idea how to operate a video camera.

Heinrich professed himself surprised by the fact that, in the aftermath of a crime, friends and neighbors, etc., invariably expressed astonishment that the person in question had committed an atrocity, as if it were possible to see inside someone's head or stake one's life on their innocence. It really was strange, said Eva.

Heinrich said that none of us differed from the man on the radio in this respect. He felt convinced, for example, that none of us would believe him, Heinrich, capable of a flagrant breach of the law, and if he were arrested overnight for murder, it would be our voices that issued from the radio, churning out the I-just-can't-believe-its and he-couldn't-possibly-have-done-its.

My partner objected that he hadn't committed murder—that was the difference. If he were arrested tomorrow and she were speaking on the radio, her statement that Heinrich was incapable of murder would be true because he genuinely hadn't committed one.

How could she be so sure? Heinrich retorted with a grin.

He was starting again, Eva exclaimed, and he'd promised to curb his tasteless witticisms.

Heinrich said he was only joking, but the underlying circumstances were serious and worthy of discussion. How did my partner know he wasn't a murderer? he demanded. It was just the same with the man's friend on the radio. Eva started to protest, but my partner interjected that Heinrich was right; one could never tell.

Meanwhile, we had reached the Stubenrauchs'. With all due care, Heinrich coasted to a stop in front of the house and we got out. Ominous storm clouds were gathering on the horizon, but the sun overhead was still generating intense heat. While feeling in his pockets for the front door key, Heinrich asked whether it was worth playing a game of badminton. It was 1:42 p.m. The press conference was scheduled to start at 3:00 and might be shown live on television.

At this point, the farmer came rushing out of the house next door. They've caught him, he hollered, they've caught him, have you heard?

Heinrich confirmed that we were in the picture and asked if there was any more news of the killer. The farmer said he didn't know, he'd only heard of the arrest. Heinrich referred him to the impending press conference, but the farmer didn't take this in. Instead, he called the prisoner a monster and a swine, etc., said they should give him short shrift, and promised to sign the petition for a referendum on the death penalty.

He also ignored Eva's inquiry as to how his wife was feeling. After a brief conversation about the weather, he turned and strode back to his house. Heinrich asked Eva how she could ask such stupid questions; it was obvious that the man had already stabbed or at least shot his wife, and she was now lying in the kitchen in her own blood. Eva punched him hard in the back and said she'd had enough of his disgusting jokes. Laughing, Heinrich unlocked the front door.

Eva immediately betook herself to the bathroom.

My partner and Heinrich pushed their way into the living room, where they jocularly contested a comfortable seat on the sofa. Heinrich argued that it was his regular place. My partner countered that she was a guest and that her wishes must be duly respected; she wanted to lie down for a brief rest, being afflicted with the fatigue that invariably beset her after an ample meal. Heinrich retorted that she could forget about having a rest, as they would soon be playing badminton. My partner greeted this statement with groans and laughter. Heinrich eventually surrendered the sofa to her, but not without adding that she would be permitted only five minutes' relaxation.

He turned on the television. "Man under interrogation. The young Styrian who was captured after a breakneck car chase is currently being questioned by the police. Press conference scheduled for 3:00 p.m. The chancellor calls for calm. No vigilantism!"

Just imagine what would happen, said Heinrich, if the man under arrest were handed over to the inhabitants of the victims' hometown. The result would be quite terrible. They would rip the eyes from his living, breathing body and subject him to every imaginable form of torture.

My partner, who was stretched out on the sofa with a hand over her eyes, told him in a low voice to desist from such descriptions.

Heinrich loudly rejoined that she mustn't take it into her head to go to sleep. Yesterday it had been she who tried to prevent Eva from going to bed by arguing how seldom we all got together. Anyway, he could hear the toilet being flushed, and that was the signal for badminton. My partner said he was awful, but she sat up and rubbed her eyes.

Heinrich called to Eva, saying that she was bound to have made a stink in the bathroom and should open the window.

The target of his injunction came into the living room. Shaking her head, she said he must be suffering from brain fever, his behavior was so appalling. He seemed to be losing his wits. What manners, what idiocy! Were we really going to play badminton? she asked. If so, she must get the picnic basket ready.

Yes, Heinrich told her, but we would only have until shortly before 3:00 p.m.

Eva laughed and tapped her forehead. If we were going to play at all, she said, we would do so properly; our game was not going be cut short by some stupid press conference. She strode firmly into the kitchen to organize the drinks. Heinrich glanced at me with a smile that implied he didn't consider the last word about the press conference to have been spoken.

My partner helped Eva to get the wicker basket ready. Heinrich and I got out the badminton net, shuttlecocks, and rackets. We took up our position outside the house. It was becoming steadily sultrier. Heinrich pointed to the clouds, which were growing ever darker. Perhaps we would be in luck, he said, and the storm would curtail our game at 2:55.

Catching sight of the fancy-dress cat in the shade of the Stubenrauchs' car, he cautiously approached the animal in order to stroke it and, so he said, divest it of its idiotic ruff and the rest of its apparel. Before he got close enough, however, the cat darted away from the car and hunkered down in the grass some twenty-five feet from us. On your own head be it, said Heinrich.

He was reminded of a children's book in which some youngsters tormented a cat by tying a tin can filled with pebbles to its tail. The cat had fled from the resulting din—to no avail, of course—but it had gone mad and eventually died. Children are brutes, he said with a laugh.

Eva had overheard the last words as she emerged from the house. Coming over to us, picnic basket in hand, she called Heinrich a monster; he was clearly incapable of thinking of anything other than atrocities and horror stories. This tickled him.

In atonement, he volunteered to carry the picnic basket, although he was already carrying the rackets. Eva handed him the basket without a word. Just as silently, but with a grin, he passed it on to me. I unresistingly took the basket in which, on top of the blanket familiar to me from the previous day, lay bottles of lemonade and mineral water and some sandwiches wrapped in aluminum foil.

However, this prompted Eva to move away from Heinrich with a disgruntled air. She tried to take the basket from me, but

I declined her offer. She called Heinrich impossible. He laughed and tried to put his arm around her, but she eluded him, so he asked me to give the basket back and apologized.

For my part, I refused to surrender the basket, because I wanted to make myself useful. Consequently, when my partner emerged from the house, she encountered three people whose intentions were diametrically opposed. She laughingly pointed this out, thereby bringing Heinrich and Eva to their senses, and they allowed me to carry the basket.

On the way to our makeshift badminton court, Eva gave vent to fears that we would not be able to play for long. The storm clouds were rapidly approaching. My partner said we must take things as they came, and we should simply start playing.

Heinrich and I put up the net. We marked out the court with discarded articles of clothing and broken twigs stuck in the ground (those of the previous day that had been dislodged by the wind or the nocturnal rainstorm). We also flattened the grass at the edge of the court by treading it down.

The wicker basket was unpacked by my partner and Eva. My partner extolled the fact that our short walk there had refreshed her and said we should at once devote the time that remained before the storm broke to playing doubles. We duly did so. Team Heinrich/self beat Team Eva/my partner 15:6. Heinrich pronounced this pointless; the difference in level of ability was too glaring. So we changed partners. My partner and I were narrowly defeated (11:15) by the Stubenrauchs.

The court was now in shadow. Heinrich wanted to make a bet as to when it would start to rain. However, the imminence of the rain was so obvious that no one took him up on it. All four of us sat down on the blanket. We refreshed ourselves with mineral water and ate our sandwiches. Heinrich and I warmly thanked the womenfolk for making the latter.

Eva rested her head against Heinrich's shoulder. Would he now be a good boy and spare their guests his black humor? she asked him.

Heinrich, with an expressionless face, called this emotional blackmail. He took a bite out of his sandwich and said, with his mouth full, that he would think it over. Eva sighed.

Big, fat raindrops began to fall. Haste was advisable, so we quickly gathered up our things. It was now as dark as it would have been at approximately 7:00 p.m. on a fine evening. Heinrich whispered to me on the way home. Hadn't he said as much?

It was 2:50 p.m. and the press conference was saved.

As soon as we were back in the dry house, the women saw to the wicker basket and its contents. Carelessly depositing the badminton net and rackets on the freezer in the hall, Heinrich hurried into the living room. I followed him. He already had the remote control in his hand and was about to turn on the television when it occurred to him to inquire if I would care for something to drink. I asked for a glass of lemonade. He got up and brought me what I'd requested, having also fetched a bottle of beer for himself. Then he turned on the television.

None of the news channels said anything about the press conference being transmitted live, but Heinrich was excited by a ticker headline: "Man Arrested Not the Killer." Following this: "The twenty-four-year-old man detained after a hectic car chase is very probably not the murderer, said a police spokesman. It was a false trail. The young man has been cleared by several witnesses."

It wasn't him, Heinrich called into the kitchen.

Eva and my partner came hurrying in.

It wasn't him, Heinrich repeated.

Wasn't it? Eva asked, and Heinrich said, No, it wasn't.

The news reported that the young man had been missing since Thursday night and was consequently under suspicion. It now turns out that the twenty-four-year-old had been barhopping since Thursday. This had been confirmed by several people who saw him at an inn at the time of the Friday killings. On his own submission, the young man fled from the police because his license had been revoked for drunk driving. He had nonetheless driven his father's car from inn to inn and was under the impression that the police wanted to arrest him for that reason.

Heinrich said the police were a bunch of morons.

The twenty-four-year-old wasn't very smart either, my partner interjected; on the contrary, the whole story sounded very depressing, poor devil.

Eva laughingly agreed.

It was interesting nonetheless, said Heinrich; now they would have to go on looking.

A new lead. The police spokesman stated that this was an unimportant setback and the noose around the killer was tightening. The twenty-four-year-old was only one suspect, and not the chief one. A successful conclusion to the manhunt may be imminent.

They won't find a soul, said Heinrich. Eva asked why he was so annoyed. Heinrich condemned the incompetence of people who allowed a murderer to roam around on the loose. He took a swig of beer and shook his head. Chuckling, he said he was going to tell their neighbor to reload his rifle. Eva gave him a warning glance.

Silence fell.

My partner drew our attention to the impressive amounts of rain falling outside. Eva shivered. Heinrich rubbed her arms and told her to shut the window. My partner wanted it left open, saying she liked the sound and the atmosphere it created. For all that, she added, she had a bad feeling—a sinister presentiment—though she couldn't be more precise about its nature.

Another silence fell.

Eva asked whether we felt like a hot meal tonight or if bread, spreads, eggs, and smoked ham would suffice. After a while, Heinrich said he didn't mind. My partner said a cold buffet would be quite enough, and I seconded her.

Because none of us could bestir ourselves sufficiently to engage in conversation or some other form of activity, Heinrich turned back to the television. This time, the women raised no objection.

Several channels were transmitting live reports from Frauenkirchen, which was also affected by rain. Heinrich switched to the channel that had broadcast the murder video the previous night. There too a reporter was speaking from the victims' hometown. Standing beneath a big umbrella, he stated that, at this moment, while a positively biblical tempest was descending on the sorely afflicted community like a sign from heaven, the police were seeking a definite suspect in the vicinity. The trail was warm, it had been announced, and the reporter added his personal opinion: In conversation with a senior police officer, he had gained the impression that the police were very sure of themselves this time.

Heinrich said he could hardly wait.

Back at the studio, the anchorwoman referred to the protests against the transmission of the murder video. The broadcasters had handled the subject responsibly, she claimed. They had received endorsements and other favorable responses from various quarters. They had asked themselves what had happened within the Austrian community and whether everyone was fully aware of it. At a time of alarming moral decline, when human life was merely a statistical quantity that was devaluing every day, people should display the courage shown by those in charge of the TV station. It had been, and still was, their duty to publicize the full dimensions of the crime.

At this point, reference was made to the station's fundraising drive for the benefit of the bereaved, whose account number was given. There followed a brief summary of what had happened.

They're like a dog with a bone, said Heinrich.

The screen was now showing some shots of Frauenkirchen. A spokesman briefly recapitulated the course of events. His report finally reached the point at which reference was made to the murders themselves. This child was doomed to die, he said. In slow motion, with the original soundtrack replaced by unearthly music, we were shown a long shot of the weeping, snot-nosed, gap-toothed brother up the tree. The music steadily increased in volume and became more dramatic the longer the shot lasted. An account number appeared.

After some three minutes, another patch of forest came into view. The death of the second boy was imminent. To the same unearthly music, the despairing face of the long-haired brother was shown as he crouched in the tree with his eyes screwed up and his chin adorned with snot and saliva. Once more, the music rose in a dramatic crescendo until Eva, when the account number was inserted, asked Heinrich to change channels or, better still, to turn off the television altogether. Heinrich complied without hesitation.

They would stop at nothing, he said; showing something like that at this time was the bitter end.

My partner went over to the window and looked out.

Heinrich stared into space, cracking his knuckles occasionally. After about five minutes, he suggested a game of table tennis. Eva didn't feel like it. Neither did my partner, who went to the table to light a cigarette and returned to the window.

After another five minutes or so, Heinrich said we could always play rummy. Thirty or forty seconds elapsed before Eva replied that she had no objection. Heinrich called to my partner to tear herself away from the window and join in. She nodded and returned to the table. I also announced my willingness to play.

Eva stood up and went to get the playing cards, which she deposited on the table with a weary gesture. Then she went out. Heinrich called after her. Where was she off to? he demanded. She was only fetching a jacket, she replied. She was back within two minutes.

Heinrich had meantime gotten out the cards, together with paper and a ballpoint pen for keeping the score. After we had been playing for around twenty minutes (Eva was in the lead, followed by me, my partner, and Heinrich, in that order), we heard a voice ring out outside. It grew louder. My partner, who had been hunched over the low coffee table while playing, straightened up and asked whom it could be. Her question was promptly answered: The voice was now coming from inside the house.

Moments later, the Stubenrauchs' farmer neighbor strode into the living room, heedless of the fact that the filth on his rubber boots was soiling the wooden floor. Had we heard? he asked, looking at Heinrich. That youngster wasn't the killer, he went on, waving his arms about. He'd thought as much—it couldn't have been anyone from around here. He'd heard it on the radio it wasn't that boy.

Heinrich asked if there was any new information.

It wasn't that youngster, the farmer reiterated; that had been obvious from the outset. How could they have gone and arrested a young man from the neighborhood?

Heinrich inquired whether the farmer had spoken with his friend in the police. The farmer said they might never catch the killer, who was bound to be long gone. Heinrich rose and towed the farmer outside, saying that he had to show him something; he didn't know how to carry out a certain repair to the house.

After the two of them had left the living room, my partner expressed surprise that the farmer had simply breezed into the house like that.

It was the custom around here and far from unusual, Eva replied. One morning shortly after they'd moved in, when Heinrich was still on leave because of the move, they were in bed together. Suddenly, the bedroom door opened to reveal the postman standing there. It'd taken them an embarrassing few seconds to disentangle themselves and pull up the bedclothes. The postman hadn't turned a hair. Far from beating an apologetic retreat, he'd handed over a certified letter and, in the overly loud voice typical of the locality, insisted on Heinrich signing for it. Heinrich blew a gasket, said Eva; he got out of bed and signed for the letter stark naked. As if that were not enough, the postman had spent a while talking, in his uncouth voice, about their move and the characteristics of the local weather at various times of year. He had also introduced himself and, with an eye to business, drawn their attention to his private poultry farm. Then, and only then, had he finally left the bedroom and the house.

My partner inquired if the postman had displayed any other signs of mental derangement. None, Eva replied; such behavior was quite customary here. Workmen, chimney sweeps, mayors, sports clubs, brass bands, ticket sellers for the firemen's ball—all entered without knocking. If they found no one in the living room or kitchen, they blithely combed the whole house without evil intent.

My partner said she wouldn't stand for such behavior; in the Stubenrauchs' place, she would keep the front door locked at all times.

That would be unthinkable, Eva rejoined; such a step would cause people in the district to promptly infer either that they, the Stubenrauchs, had something to hide or that they didn't feel part of the local community. Both inferences would entail certain disadvantages, principal among which were social ostracism and the withholding of neighborly assistance. In this neck of the woods, said Eva, you have to run with the pack.

Heinrich came back into the house and took off his shoes. Looking into the living room, he swore at the dirt on the floor and went to fetch a mop. In a low voice, Eva asked if he had managed to shake the farmer off. He mopped the floor with gritted teeth until the sweat stood out on his forehead.

Hadn't he done well? he demanded, smiling at us. By showing the farmer a hole in the gutter, he had given him something to worry about and distracted him from his tirades. Eva hoped Heinrich hadn't been unfriendly. He had combined cunning with tact, he replied; the farmer would have nothing to reproach him for. Eva manifested relief at this. She was the one that spent the most time with these people and had to get on with them, she said, being at home while Heinrich was at work.

Heinrich asked if we could go on playing. My partner fetched two packets of chips and two bottles of mineral water from the kitchen. Depositing them all on the coffee table, she said, Yes, she was ready. We went on with our game.

After we had played three more hands, the telephone rang. Grumbling, Heinrich searched around for his shoes, which the involuntary movements of his feet had pushed in different directions beneath the table, then jumped up and hurried out into the passage.

While he was speaking with the person on the other end of the line, my partner reverted to the subject of lack of privacy. She asked why people should consider it so reprehensible of someone to keep their house locked up during the day. After all, everyone agreed that half of the rest of the world's inhabitants were a bad lot. Why should it be any different here? Eva said she didn't know, but now that unheralded visits from neighbors no longer made her feel uneasy, or she had gotten used to them, she had stopped thinking of locking the front door.

Unpleasant situations were rare. Indeed, if she discounted the postman's intrusion, she could think of only one other incident that had unnerved her. On one occasion, one of the African immigrants who roamed around with self-produced and terribly ugly paintings had walked into the house when she was on her own there. Most of these men were students, she said. They went from house to house, mainly in rural areas, offering their little works of art for sale.

Some days before the visit in question, there had been a press report that Africans had committed two rapes in Graz, so the black picture-seller's entrance had made her nervous. As a rule, she always gave such people something. This time, she had told him she was poor and he should leave. He'd laughed at her and said she had nice hair. Where was her husband?

That really alarmed her. He was working upstairs, she'd replied. The picture-seller laughed again and said he didn't believe her; she was all on her own, and he'd appreciate something to eat and drink. Under other circumstances, said Eva, she would have given him something, but because she found him frightening, she told him to leave.

He'd started on again about her husband's absence, however. This had caused Eva to leave the house and request assistance from their neighbor, who was strolling around his farmyard. On seeing the farmer, the picture-seller had promptly fled without trying to interest him or his wife in a picture.

So my partner could see, Eva concluded, that being embedded in the rural social structure has definite advantages.

My partner, who was about to raise some objection, was interrupted by an exclamation from Heinrich. We listened. He kept saying, aha, yes, so that's the way it is.

Just as my partner was about to respond once more, Heinrich hung up and hurried into the room. The podiatrist had called, he said, but first he needed a drink. He poured himself a glass of wine from a bottle that had been standing around since the previous night.

The podiatrist? asked Eva.

Heinrich nodded. Yes, he said, the podiatrist they'd patronized several times since living in the district had called. Some thirty policemen and paramilitaries had passed her house, guns at the ready and heading north. Heinrich surveyed us expectantly.

My partner asked what he inferred from this. Where did the podiatrist live and what lay north of there?

Heinrich took a map from some wooden shelves in the corner. Back at the table, he lit a cigarette although he already had one smoldering in the ashtray. Unfolding the map, he said it was the most detailed graphic representation of the area obtainable; indeed, he doubted if even the CIA possessed a better one. He spread the map out on the table (actually, he held it in his hands for a while until we had cleared away playing cards, glasses, bottles, paper and pencils, cigarettes, ashtrays, etc.).

Then he asked Eva for the pen and drew a line. This is where the podiatrist lives, he said. He had gotten her to describe precisely which way the police were headed and where they had turned, etc., so he was able to plot their route with great accuracy. He extended the line on the map and said, This is where we live, here in the north, then drew a circle around the Stubenrauchs' house.

My partner asked how far apart the houses were. A mile or two, Heinrich replied.

You mean they're coming here? my partner exclaimed. Is the murderer roaming around in this area? Her voice broke.

Heinrich said it didn't amount to anything yet, but first he wanted to have a word with the farmer and instruct him to ask his acquaintances in the district by phone if they had observed any unusual police activity. He himself would do likewise, though he didn't know many people around here. Meanwhile, we could listen to the radio and look at the news on online.

Just as Heinrich rose, we heard the neighbor's voice outside the door. Once again, he came stomping into the living room in his rubber boots. He told us that a Herr Zach had called him and reported that a horde of policemen had tramped through his farmyard. They were heading for the property of the Weber family, not far from here.

Great excitement reigned in the room.

This is it, said my partner.

Heinrich picked up the map. Going over to the farmer, he asked him if he could point out or mark Herr Zach's farm and the Weber family's property with the pen. The farmer held the map away from him and squinted at it, then took it over to the window, with the result that his huge, gnarled, filth-encrusted hands and his equally huge, black fingernails were clearly visible.

Eva quietly remarked that it had stopped raining.

What did you say? asked Heinrich.

In the same tone of voice, Eva repeated that it had stopped raining.

Lucky for the policemen, Heinrich said casually.

He once more asked the farmer if he could indicate a definite location. Being unable to read a map, he couldn't. Laboriously, Heinrich showed him which house lay where and which places, roads, and hills were shown. In that way, he managed to give the farmer an approximate idea of what the map conveyed. The man took the pen and drew on the map.

Heinrich came back to the table. With the aid of finger movements and oral explanations, he made it clear that the two police contingents so far identified were moving toward each other and said that the Stubenrauchs' house lay roughly on their line of convergence. My partner sprang to her feet without uttering a word or doing anything else. It was evident that the situation Heinrich had described alarmed her. It didn't really mean anything, said Heinrich; on the contrary, it was highly amusing.

About to add something, he was interrupted by the entrance of the farmer's wife. She said a brief hello, then breathlessly informed her husband that the mayor had called to say he couldn't get through.

The mayor? said the farmer.

Yes, she replied, Hans Fleck.

He called? said the farmer.

Yes, she replied, he can't get through.

Get through where? asked the farmer.

By car, she replied.

Heinrich intervened. Had the mayor really called and what exactly had he said? The farmer's wife replied that he had called to say he'd meant to drive to Farmer Kienreich's, which was only a third of a mile from here, but a police roadblock had held him up—him, the mayor. The whole area was cordoned off. The murderer was being sought here. Even the mayor himself had been prevented from driving on. He had called to tell the farmer to lock his door, and everyone in the area should do likewise. It was outrageous that nothing had been said on the radio.

Frozen-faced, my partner demanded that we leave at once by car. She had no wish to stay here, she said. Before I could reply, Heinrich told her she was being absurd. In the first place, a single individual posed very little threat to the persons assembled here. Secondly, she ought to ask herself if she wouldn't have to summon up even more courage to drive along deserted roads under potential threat from the camera killer. And thirdly, she mustn't leave him and Eva all on their own. This he said with a smile. My partner sighed and rolled her eyes.

Heinrich urged us all to remain calm. The farmer and his wife should go home and endeavor to obtain more information, for instance by calling acquaintances nearby. After a while, in half an hour or so, our two groups would meet again, either here or next door, to exchange news. He didn't care where this council of war took place, but if their neighbors came here, he could offer them a glass of the excellent apricot brandy he and Eva had recently been given. The farmer pronounced himself in full agreement and promised to return with his wife after making a few phone calls.

When the couple had left, Heinrich locked the front door and picked up the phone.

My partner was seated in her armchair, pale-faced. She said she felt terribly nervous and didn't even dare to go over to the window, for if she suddenly caught sight of a stranger on the road, she would very probably have a heart attack. Furthermore, she thoroughly disapproved of Heinrich telephoning outside in the hall. In the event of a surprise attack by the camera killer, who might be intending to take hostages and film them or escape with their assistance, we should all stay close together for mutual support.

Eva strove to calm her down. She pointed out that Heinrich was only some twenty feet away and drew attention to her husband's immense physical strength. The camera killer would be well advised to give the house a wide berth, she said. At all events, she herself wasn't frightened. And now she was going to the kitchen to brew some coffee. She was expecting guests. Someone in this madhouse had to keep a sense of perspective, and that was clearly her own allotted role.

When Eva got to her feet, my partner caught hold of her. She wanted everyone to stay together, she said.

Eva: Very well, why not simply come too?

My partner agreed on the condition that I accompany her. I did as I was bidden.

As we made our way along the hall in single file, Heinrich, who had evidently overheard our conversation, tapped his forehead and laughed. We heard him explaining the situation on the phone and asking someone for information about police movements.

In the kitchen, Eva filled a kettle with water and urged my partner to sit down. My partner refused on the grounds that, theoretically, just theoretically, someone seated at the table would make an easier target. She preferred to stand up against the wall, she said. Eva went over to my partner, put her arms around her, and argued that no such danger impended.

My partner said she had a nasty feeling, a sinister presentiment. Eva insisted that the camera killer hadn't become notorious for his use of firearms; all he had done was threaten some little children with a knife, and knives didn't fly through closed windows. Eva's remarks were sporadically punctuated or accompanied by exclamations from Heinrich that threatened to neutralize their soothing effect, so she shut the door to the hall.

No, please don't, cried my partner, only to laugh at herself a moment later—an activity (laughter) in which Eva joined. Visibly summoning up all her willpower, my partner sat down at the table.

Eva pointed out that she had a good view of the neighbors' house and its front door from there; perhaps that would reassure her somewhat. My partner shrugged her shoulders, smiling forlornly.

We listened as the sound of boiling water increased in volume. Then the kettle emitted a whistle. Just as Eva removed it from the stove and poured its contents onto the coffee powder in the pot, Heinrich came in brandishing the map. The situation was all very exciting and becoming steadily more so, he said. Had we listened to the radio?

Eva said no. My partner begged Heinrich not to keep her on tenterhooks.

He announced that he had unashamedly called various people he'd spoken to only two or three times at most, having had to look up their numbers in the telephone directory. In view of the prevailing emergency, however, it had been easy to talk with them. Everyone was eager to exchange views with other people, and many phone numbers were engaged; the camera killer was clearly generating a lot of business for the post office this afternoon.

If he didn't come out with it at once, said my partner, she would go mad.

Heinrich laughed. To cut a long story short, he said, it seemed we were surrounded.

What? my partner cried.

He repeated that there was some evidence that we, or the area in which the Stubenrauchs' residence happened to be situated, had been encircled. My partner requested him to quickly give us a brief but more detailed explanation. Heinrich sat down, spread out the map on the table, and picked up a pen. According to his information, he said, police were stationed here (he made a mark) and were advancing (he drew an arrow) in this direction. They were also here, here, and here. At every "here," he made another mark on the map. The marks formed a circle, which he joined up with the ballpoint. What was more, said Eva, the circle was getting smaller.

Resting the elbow of her right arm on Heinrich's shoulder, she remarked that the police really did seem to be looking for the killer nearby.

It gets even more interesting, said Heinrich. His telephone calls had been extremely illuminating. Wild rumors were circulating. A garage mechanic's wife with whom he had spoken claimed to have definitely heard shots in the woods adjoining her property. Other people had indirectly confirmed this by asserting that the murderer was being hunted in the Lechnerwald, a wooded area thirty or forty acres in extent and known by the name of its owner, a Herr Lechner.

Someone else had also testified to hearing shots. Against this, the story of the shots had been consigned to the realm of fantasy by a restaurateur whose gastronomic establishment was situated only a hundred yards from the garage mechanic's house. He did not, however, hesitate to concede that he was hard of hearing; moreover, he had been busy tasting wine in the cellar and might have been distracted thereby.

Summing up, Heinrich said that the modus operandi adopted by the police made an uncoordinated and ill-considered impression—unless, of course, they knew precisely where the killer was. If he were definitely in a cordoned-off patch of forest (e.g., the aforementioned Lechnerwald), their initiative was to be welcomed, but if the authorities merely surmised him to be somewhere inside the circle on the map, the devil was in the details.

In fact, it wasn't out of the question that my partner's presentiment would prove correct: If cornered, the killer might take a hostage. However, nothing was known for certain.

Personally, said Heinrich, he now believed that the man was not in the vicinity.

At that moment, my partner, staring stiffly out the window, declared that she couldn't believe her eyes. We went over to her. Despite this, my partner behaved as if she had to tell us what she was seeing. The farmer was coming out of his house with his wife and a great big rifle in his hands, she said, ready to fire.

Here comes Rambo! cried Heinrich. How nice, we were going to have guests or reinforcements, whichever, and my partner ought to be pleased.

She, however, stated that she wouldn't remain in the same room as that madman, not at any price; he was quite capable of blazing away in all directions. At any rate, he shouldn't be offered any hard liquor.

Heinrich did not appear to take my partner's misgivings very seriously. He went to the front door and opened it. As before, the farmer omitted to remove his boots. He marched into the kitchen complete with hat, jacket, overalls, boots, and the rifle on his shoulder. We greeted him. He sat down, emitting a distinctly flatulent expulsion of wind as he did so.

His wife handed Eva a circular tin approximately ten inches in diameter and filled with cookies, saying that it would provide us with something to eat. Eva replied that it wasn't necessary but thanked her warmly and invited her to sit down; coffee would be served at once.

Heinrich deposited a schnapps glass and a bottle filled with transparent liquid in front of the farmer. Heedless of my partner's dissuasive gestures, he invited him to help himself. The farmer wasted no time in doing so, remarking—without a smile—that it would improve his aim. Well done, my partner told Heinrich in an undertone, failing to grasp that she could be heard all over the room.

Heinrich informed the farmer of what he had managed to learn on the phone. The farmer's wife appeared to have conducted the phone calls to their neighbors. She spoke of similar matters but added that a house search was rumored to have been carried out in an unidentified location in the vicinity.

Heinrich turned on the kitchen radio and resumed his seat. The farmer spoke for the first time: He requested Heinrich to turn off the radio on the grounds that we would fail to hear what was happening outside the house. Heinrich complied, saying that the radio wouldn't broadcast an all clear, in any case.

Eva, who had poured everyone a second cup of coffee by now, passed the cookies around again. While doing so, she extolled their quality and inquired if the farmer's wife had baked them herself. The farmer's wife confirmed this. She and Eva exchanged opinions on the correct way of making various desserts.

The farmer, who refused to be parted from his rifle even when seated, drank a second apricot brandy. Then he wiped his lips on the sleeve of his jacket and indulged in some uncouth behavior (ordering his wife to keep her voice down, peremptorily requesting Heinrich to open the window, saying that one could never tell and he wanted to hear and be prepared). My partner sighed and rose to her feet. Heinrich opened the window. It was quite evident that he was smiling, apparently not offended by the farmer's brusque manner.

Eva succeeded in engaging my partner in a conversation about various aspects of cuisine, with the result that, after a minute or two, her face relaxed to such an extent that a timid smile became discernible.

Heinrich said he had to fetch something and left the kitchen. Before closing the door, he gave me a surreptitious signal to follow him. I obeyed his invitation.

Before I had even reached the door, my partner hailed me. What was I up to and where was I going?

I replied that I had to go to the bathroom, if I might be so permitted. My remark evoked reactions ranging from grins to laughter from all present, even the farmer, who was still sitting there with his hat on.

Heinrich was waiting for me in the hall. He was feeling tense, he whispered, and this coffee party didn't appeal to him. He wanted to go outside and take a look—see where the police were prowling around and how far away they were. Would I come with him?

I agreed to, but pointed out that our plan was bound to meet with my partner's disapproval. She had more than once expressed the wish that we all stay together. Moreover, she disagreed with the presence of the armed and schnapps-drinking farmer. If we were not there, I said, she might find him even more of a threat.

Heinrich conceded this. He propped his chin on his fist. After a while, he said he had found the answer. We should explain that we wanted to clarify the situation by speaking with the police in person. I didn't consider this the best plan possible, I said, but it was worth a try.

I followed Heinrich into the living room. He turned on the television news, then switched from channel to channel. On one channel, we saw a helicopter shot of the area in which we ourselves were located. Fancy that, said Heinrich.

A subtitle stated that the report was coming live from West Styria. Heinrich said we ought soon to set off to speak with the police; we could watch the rest on television later. We had better not mention this broadcast to my partner, he added; it might make her nervous.

I agreed.

We went back into the kitchen. In the doorway, we nearly bumped into the farmer. He had his gun on his shoulder and was trying to get past us. Heinrich inquired where he was going. The farmer said he intended to take up his post outside and lie in wait for the killer. Heinrich let him go.

When the door had closed behind the farmer, Heinrich jokingly asked his wife how much liquor her husband could take before he lost control over his trigger finger. Unsmiling, she declared that her husband could take a great deal, had hardly touched a drop, and there was no need to worry—for us, at least, though the killer had better watch his step.

Outside the house, the farmer was gesticulating and calling something to us. We couldn't understand him because my partner had shut the window again after his exit. Heinrich went out into the yard. We already knew what he had to tell us when he returned because we could hear it ourselves: A helicopter was thundering overhead. Heinrich said he proposed to go with me and look for the police.

Predictably enough, my partner vetoed this. What was that supposed to mean? she demanded; it was out of the question.

Heinrich said it was urgently necessary for us to speak with the police. Did she want to sit there quaking with fear for hours in ignorance of what was really happening?

No, said my partner, she didn't, but the idea of sitting there all by herself appealed to her even less.

She wouldn't be sitting there all by herself, Heinrich retorted; Eva and the lady from next door were there too. As for personal protection, their resolute and courageous neighbor outside was the most suitable man for the purpose.

It was noticeable that this very argument aroused mixed feelings in my partner. Doubtless from a sense of discretion, however, she refrained from informing his wife of her misgivings about the man patrolling outside the front door.

So Heinrich slipped on his shoes and gestured me to follow his example before any further objection could be raised. We waved to the ladies left behind in the kitchen and went outside the house, where we explained our intention to the farmer. We requested him, in the event that he had to open fire, to double-check whom he was aiming at, because it might be one of us. The farmer declared that he was an experienced hunter who never missed his target and selected it with care, could tell the difference between an ibex and a stag and a stag and a man, and so on and so forth.

I followed at Heinrich's heels. In our loafers, which were not best suited to the weather conditions, and which squelched in the residual moisture left by the rainstorm, we made our way across country in the direction of our improvised badminton court. Heinrich opined that, in his estimation, that was where we could expect to encounter the nearest police unit.

It was chilly, and we both found we were dressed too lightly. This we endeavored to offset by striding out more briskly. While we were forging our way uphill through bushes and tall grass, Heinrich said he felt very tempted to play a practical joke on our return. He owned a video camera, he said. Armed with this, he proposed to appear at the kitchen window and, without revealing his identity, film the interior.

However, he doubted it would be desirable to put this idea into effect. In the first place, there was a risk that some more sensitive soul (e.g., my partner) might be genuinely traumatized. A schoolboy prank was one thing, but he had no wish to be responsible for inducing a heart attack. Secondly, it wasn't beyond the bounds of possibility that the farmer would lose his head and make use of his firearm. Both of those eventualities had to be precluded, and he supposed that was impracticable. I agreed with him.

After climbing the hill, we looked around us in a 360-degree arc. There wasn't a soul to be seen, just a pheasant crowing and fluttering in a cornfield. Heinrich pointed to a patch of forest a half mile from our own location. That was the Lechnerwald, he said; to the best of his knowledge, the police were in there.

We debated what to do. After all, we couldn't dismiss the possibility that we might strike the police as suspicious and get into trouble. Heinrich indicated a spot not far away: the end of a row of leafy trees that led to the vicinity of the forest. If we reached that row of trees, he said, we might be able to get to the forest and, thus, to the policemen concealed within it.

I queried the necessity for these precautionary measures. After all, I said, we intended to speak with the police. Heinrich said he had completely abandoned that idea. There was no point in talking to them; they would not divulge any information to us, in any case. He thought it sufficient to locate them and deduce where they were headed and what they were up to.

I objected that this would not enable us to bring my partner the detailed information she had requested. Heinrich said he already had an idea and would think of something. I pronounced myself satisfied with this.

When we reached the row of trees, Heinrich told me to keep low. We crouched down behind a tree. From there, on a road some five hundred to six hundred yards away, we saw a police car. Where's it going? said Heinrich. Is it heading for our place? Let's see whether it turns off.

The car really was heading for the vicinity of the Stubenrauchs' residence. Instead of turning right, however, as it would have had to in order to get there, it drove straight on along the main road. From one point of view, said Heinrich, he regretted this because a visit from the guardians of the law would certainly have relieved the strain on my partner's nerves; on the other hand, a full explanation of the situation would rob it of its excitement.

He was feeling a little as he had when playing cops and robbers in his childhood. Don't laugh at me, he said, raising his voice because another helicopter—not the one we had sighted earlier—was flying past at low altitude approximately a hundred yards from us.

We made our way toward the Lechnerwald. Before we reached it, Heinrich turned to me and put a finger to his lips. We tiptoed on. Soon we heard dogs barking and, shortly thereafter, voices.

What if he waited for the policemen here, Heinrich whispered, standing with his legs apart and a video camera aimed at their advancing figures? That would give them a shock. He laughed as he said this.

Pausing behind a tree with a massive trunk, we peered in the direction from which the voices were coming. Soon afterward, we caught sight of several policemen with dogs on leashes.

Damnation, said Heinrich, they're heading this way—let's go.

I followed him back to the end of the row of trees. There he said he wanted to go reconnoitering elsewhere.

Hurriedly, we set off to the west. We had not gone far when we made out some figures in open country around a mile away. Heinrich definitely identified them as policemen. Now we knew the score, he said; either the forces of law and order were a bunch of bunglers, or the man with cinematic ambitions was hiding in the trigger-happy farmer's loft, and he considered the former alternative more likely.

He suggested we retrace our steps, notify the others, and turn on the television. I agreed, so we walked swiftly back to the Stubenrauchs' house. Around a quarter of a mile before we got there, Heinrich started calling the farmer's name lest he take fright or yield to the temptation to try out his skill as a marksman. The man waved to us when we reached the farmyard. All he had seen, he said, was two helicopters.

Heinrich told him that we had sighted a number of policemen and that it was probable we would soon be receiving visitors. Good, said the farmer; he had no wish to hang around there forever. Loudly calling out that it was us, Heinrich and I went into the house.

Eva was just replacing the telephone receiver. The phone had never stopped ringing, she said. Her mother had sent her regards and advised us all to drive to her place at once; she had been listening to the radio and watching television and was terribly alarmed. Other callers, people from the neighborhood, had asserted that the killer was in the immediate vicinity of the Stubenrauch residence. Heinrich said we would soon know or could watch ourselves on television.

He went into the living room and turned on the television. The same channel as before was still showing aerial views of the district. Policemen could be seen. The commentator was inaudible over the noise of the helicopter.

Without turning off the television, Heinrich and I went into the kitchen and poured ourselves some lemonade. White as a sheet, my partner begged us to enlighten her. What had we managed to elicit and how did things stand?

Contrary to expectation, said Heinrich, we'd had no opportunity to speak with the police but had sighted a whole host of them. My partner had no need to worry, he told her; they were obviously on their way here, so she would soon be able to speak with them herself. It genuinely seemed either that the authorities were on the wrong track or that the camera killer was very close at hand.

My partner sprang to her feet. Why don't they evacuate us? she cried. Why don't they evacuate us? Exerting considerable vocal power, she demanded that we get into our cars and leave at once. Her lips trembled and she burst into tears.

On seeing how desperate she was, we stated our willingness to do as she wished. The farmer's wife said she might leave too. On the other hand, she realized that her husband would never give way. She knew him of old; he was as stubborn as a mule, and she suspected him of planning to detain the murderer on his own initiative or put him out of action with a bullet. She would also prefer him to leave for fear of some mishap, etc., but it was no use. Heinrich and Eva said that if their neighbors were staying, we couldn't leave either.

Convince him, cried my partner, convince him.

Heinrich went outside and conveyed her request to the farmer. Through the window, we saw the latter make a dismissive gesture, point to his house, and brandish his gun. My partner dashed outside with us at her heels. She planted herself in front of the farmer and shouted at him. The loudness of her voice was doubtless dictated by agitation, but also by the proximity of the helicopters, which were making a prodigious, incessant din.

We must leave here at once, my partner cried, waving her arms and jumping up and down in front of the farmer.

He shook his head. He was staying put, he said; the rest of us should go. That was out of the question, Heinrich replied. We—he meant my partner and me—wished to leave; he and Eva were staying. We two should drive to the nearest town and wait at a hotel there. This business would soon be over, he said, and we could keep abreast of developments by telephone. I asked my trembling partner if she approved of this course of action.

Just at that moment, Eva appeared at the living room window. We must see this, she called.

Hurrying over to her, we looked through the window and saw an aerial shot of the property on television. Everyone was clearly visible: the farmer with his gun, us outside the window, the parked cars—even the dressed-up cat fleeing from the noise in terror.

Heinrich left the window. Fantastic, he said, we're on television! He hurried inside and turned on the video recorder so as to tape the broadcast. Then he rejoined us outside the house.

Look, he exclaimed, policemen!

We looked in the direction of his outstretched arm. Sure enough, a contingent of policemen with dogs was coming into view some four hundred yards away.

He's here, I tell you, my partner yelled, and she ran off toward the oncoming policemen.

Eva made to go after her, but Heinrich told her to stay where she was. My partner's nerves were completely shot, he said; if she would feel safer with the policemen, we oughtn't stop her. He added that it was annoying we couldn't hear what was being said on television because of the racket the helicopters were making.

We stood idly beside the window for a while. On the screen inside we saw my partner running toward the line of policemen, who were steadily converging.

Eva said she would bring out some drinks for us. No one else considered going back inside the house—that much was clear. Shortly after she disappeared into the building, she opened a kitchen window. We should go around the house and look in the other direction, she called. We complied with her request and were unsurprised to see dozens of policemen around two hundred yards away. They were also making straight for the properties of the Stubenrauchs and their neighbors.

We returned to the front of the house and the television window, whichever. The contingent of policemen with my partner in their midst had approached to within approximately a hundred yards. A police car could be seen on television, driving along the road with its blue lights on.

Eva came out into the yard with a tray of drinks. She had heard on the radio that the inhabitants of the district were being instructed to go into their homes and lock their doors because of the hunt for the killer. With a nervous smile, she wondered if that applied in our case. After all, she said, the forces of law and order responsible for our protection were very close at hand and present in large numbers.

Heinrich laughed. No, he replied, he thought it was permissible for us to remain outside the house. He gave the nearest helicopter a wave. I saw this on the television and turned around.

We could already make out the faces of the approaching policemen. Although with them, my partner didn't speak to anyone and remained on the sidelines. She was only wearing a T-shirt, so someone had draped a jacket around her shoulders. She was staring at the ground. The policewoman walking along close beside her was eying her with concern.

When the squad was within approximately twenty-five yards of us, it came to a halt. With a laugh, Heinrich called to my partner that all danger had been averted. He got no response, however. The body of policemen approaching from the other direction could now be seen from where we were standing. They halted about a hundred feet away.

We saw on television that the property was surrounded on all sides. The police car, lights flashing, came into view once more. The farmer asked both police contingents what was up. Were Herr Schober or Herr Haberfellner with them? One of the policemen called back, telling him to lay down his weapon at once. After some prevarication, the recipient of the order obeyed. The television deemed this incident worthy of a close-up.

The police car drove into the farmyard, siren wailing, and pulled up. The sound of the siren ceased; the blue lights continued to flash. Three policemen jumped out of the vehicle. The senior officer put his hands on his hips and surveyed his men and us in turn. I saw on the screen how Heinrich too kept turning to look at the television, on which the three policemen's intervention could be observed. The senior officer took a few steps across the yard. He appeared to be examining the license plate numbers of the cars parked there. Then he jerked his thumb at one of the vehicles and asked whom it belonged to.

Them, Heinrich told him—his guests, in other words, my partner and me. The television clearly showed him pointing us out.

The senior officer and one of his men came over to me. We've got him, he said; that's the man.

On the screen, I saw Eva, who was standing beside me with the tray, retreat several feet. Behind me, my partner started to scream. On the television, I saw handcuffs being produced and turned around. The officer in command announced that I was under arrest; I was charged with having murdered two children.

I do not deny this.

About the Author

THOMAS GLAVINIC IS CONSIDERED one of the guiding voices in Austrian literature. Born in 1972, he is the author of several novels, as well as a number of essays and short stories. His work has garnered both critical acclaim and commercial success and has been translated into sixteen languages. Glavinic worked as an advertising copywriter and taxi driver before releasing his debut novel, *Carl Haffner's Love of the Draw*, in 1998. *The Camera Killer* is his third book to be published in English. It was awarded the 2002 Friedrich-Glauser Prize for crime fiction and has been adapted for the screen. Glavinic was short-listed for the German Book Prize in 2007, and his *How to Live*, forthcoming from AmazonCrossing, reached #1 on the Austrian best-seller list.

About the Translator

ORIGINALLY A CLASSICIST WHOSE school diet from age eight included ancient Greek as well as Latin, John Brownjohn won a major scholarship to Oxford, from where he graduated with honors. Thereafter, partly because he hails from a ramified family whose members fought on both sides during World War II, he made the transition to modern languages and a career as a literary translator that has earned him critical acclaim and many British and American awards. In addition to translating the better part of two hundred books, he has produced English versions of many German and French screenplays and cowritten several feature films with Roman Polanski.